PRAISE FOR

THE TREASURE OF TUNDAVALA GAP

A Mateus de Silva Adventure

"Jeffrey K. Schmoll's novel punches like a snub-nosed .357, but in his firm grip this multigenerational, cross-cultural thriller hits its mark and promises more to come."

—Mike Maden, *New York Times* best-selling author of Tom Clancy's Jack Ryan Jr. series and Clive Cussler's Oregon Files series

"Unexpected developments, dangerous encounters, plot twists, and colorful characters give this story considerable depth and gut-wrenching emotion."

—Reedsy Discovery Reviews: 5-Star/Must-Read

"*The Treasure of Tundavala Gap* makes significant contributions to the literary world by offering a unique and thrilling adventure set in an underrepresented locale. Its potential to enthrall and educate readers while providing an entertaining and suspenseful tome is a testament to Schmoll's storytelling prowess. This book is a must-read for adventure enthusiasts and those seeking a culturally rich and immersive reading experience."

—Sally Majors, the Chrysalis BREW Project: 5-Star/
Brew Seal of Excellence

"*The Treasure of Tundavala Gap* is a pulse-pounding adventure that seamlessly blends heart-stopping action with captivating storytelling. From Cuba to Angola, this cinematic tale immerses readers in a world of high-stakes treasure hunting, danger, and unexpected twists. With its compelling characters and vividly rendered settings, Schmoll delivers a thrilling read that fans of Dan Brown and *National Treasure* won't be able to put down. An unforgettable journey from start to finish!"

—David Crow, author of the award-winning bestseller
Pale Faced Lie

"My goodness, what a roller coaster of a book! I have just finished reading this and can highly recommend it. Fans of treasure hunts and richly detailed plots will love it."

—Rachael Gray, doctor of clinical psychology, author of
A Little Bird Told Me

"Immersive and action packed from the very start. Schmoll skillfully weaves colourful timelines, compelling narratives, and on-the-edge-of-your-seat thrills to create a story in its own league entirely. A must-read for action adventure lovers!"

—Emily Quinn, Quintillion Book Reviews

"My attention was held right until the last page (especially with that cliffhanger ending!) and I never wanted it to end. This book has everything you could hope for in a thrilling adventure novel. I'm desperate for book two!"

—Charlotte Armstrong, *The Pen Not the Sword* book blog

"*The Treasure of Tundavala Gap* is a pulse-pounding adventure that sweeps readers into a world of high-stakes treasure hunting and danger. From the wilds of Africa to historical encounters with iconic figures, this novel blends heart-stopping action with captivating storytelling. With its cinematic scope and gripping plot twists, Schmoll's narrative keeps you riveted from start to finish. A must-read for fans of thrilling escapades and unforgettable journeys!"

—Bill Canady, best-selling author of *The 80/20 CEO*

"Embark on a riveting journey with *The Treasure of Tundavala Gap* as you delve into a heart-pounding tale of adventure, danger, and unyielding courage. This action-packed novel leads you through untamed territories, embroiled in the pursuit of a legendary fortune."

—Kevin Tanza, Book Nerdection: Must-Read Award

"This is a brilliant story which had me instantly turning the pages. I loved following Mateus's journey and the adventure, which kept me glued to the pages, and as a result I read this whole book in just one day! A brilliant and thrilling adventure."

—*The Strawberry Post* book blog

"*The Treasure of Tundavala Gap* by Jeffrey K. Schmoll is an enticing historical action thriller with well-developed characters."

—Susan, *Readorrot* book blog

"*The Treasure of Tundavala Gap* is a captivating tale that grabs you from the start. With every twist in Mateus and his companions' quest for a legendary fortune, the tension rises. This thrilling story of danger and unexpected turns is a delight for fans of love and adventure!"

—Todd Hugie, author of *The House Down Dirt Lane*

"*The Treasure of Tundavàla Gap* is a moving, rollicking, breathtaking, page-turning adventure. Jeffrey K. Schmoll whisks the reader from Cuba to Angola to Namibia to California, following tech nerds, rebels, expert gamers, gangsters, and generals, all in pursuit of precious Angolan diamonds. Schmoll's three main characters immediately grab the reader's interest and sympathy. He expertly brings to life the novel's multiple settings, especially Angola, which Schmoll portrays with particular and compelling care. After five pages, I was hooked and couldn't put it down. Hopefully, Schmoll will give us the sequel he hints at. I'll be waiting."

—Philip Graubart, author of *Here There Is No Why* and *Women and God*

The Treasure of Tundavala Gap
by Jeffrey K Schmoll

© Copyright 2024 Jeffrey K Schmoll

979-8-88824-463-0

FICTION

All rights reserved. No part of this publication may be reproduced, stored in a retrieval system, or transmitted in any form or by any means—electronic, mechanical, photocopy, recording, or any other—except for brief quotations in printed reviews, without the prior written permission of the author.

This is a work of fiction. All the characters in this book are fictitious, and any resemblance to actual persons, living or dead, is purely coincidental. The names, incidents, dialogue, and opinions expressed are products of the author's imagination and are not to be construed as real.

Cover design by Suzanne Bradshaw.

Published by

köehlerbooks™

3705 Shore Drive
Virginia Beach, VA 23455
800-435-4811
www.koehlerbooks.com

THE TREASURE OF TUNDAVALA GAP

A Mateus de Silva Adventure

JEFFREY K SCHMOLL

VIRGINIA BEACH
CAPE CHARLES

To the warm-hearted people of Angola, forever in my heart, and to the dedicated engineers and colleagues working in Cabinda and the Chicala office.
Muito Obrigado.

"My Heart Breathes"
(sung in Chokwe)

Muono wange huima,	(My heart breathes,)
Huima muono wange,	(My heart breathes,)
Keti uzuzukue,	(Don't lose your morale,)
Muno wante wa MPLA.	(For my life belongs to the MPLA.)

CHAPTER 1
SOMEONE ELSE'S BATTLE

Cuanza Sul Province, Angola, March 21, 1984

The radio crackled with panicked shouts as Colonel Juan Mateus de Silva's gaze swept across the makeshift command tent, his heart heavy with the weight of impending doom. The Cuban radioman turned, sweat beading on his brow. "Second rifle unit is not responding, *mi Coronel.*"

Another burst of static and the sound of panicked shouts. "First rifles being pushed back. Second armor in full retreat!"

De Silva's jaw clenched, his blue eyes flashing with frustration. They were being routed by the enemy UNITA forces entrenched on the high ground of the Cuanza Sul Province in Angola.

Without hesitation, de Silva barked orders, his voice cutting through the chaos in the tent. "Deploy Second infantry west toward the left flank. Send Third and Fourth rifles north to the center. *Ándale!*"

The radioman's fingers flew across the dials. "*Sí, Coronel!*" His words tense and rushed as he shouted into the battered green microphone, relaying de Silva's commands to the front lines.

Two radios blared with incomprehensible shouts in Spanish and Portuguese, interspersed with the staccato roar of explosions. One radio linked them to the overall command, while the other communicated their own beleaguered Fifth Company movements.

An inexperienced Angolan comms runner cowered in the corner, hands over his ears to block out the terrifying sounds. He was there to run orders out into the field but wasn't ready to go anywhere right now, knees shaking and eyes closed.

De Silva's presence filled the tent, his neatly pressed Cuban Revolutionary Army fatigues like a second skin, three yellow stars of a *primer coronel* or senior colonel glinting on his shoulders. He exuded a warrior's belief in the mission, which permeated the space and gave confidence to his men. But inside, his gut twisted. Losing his men was unthinkable, unbearable. His aide, Major Maceo Perez stood to his right and slightly behind, just as powerless as de Silva to stop the carnage.

"Comms runner!" De Silva's voice cut through the chaos. The young Angolan runner trembled, eyes wide with primal fear, rooted in place. Sweat poured from his face as he willed himself to be anyplace else. De Silva moved toward the man, gripped his shoulder, and spoke into his ear.

"We all feel the fear . . . all of us, my brother. You can do this." Despite the bullets, the bombs, and the screams from an adjacent medical tent, the comms runner straightened, a new purpose in his eyes.

De Silva spoke loudly for all to hear, "Runner. Second Infantry to the left flank."

"*Sí, mi Coronel!*" The comms runner sprinted out of the tent, his fear forgotten or at least held at bay as he ran into war.

De Silva turned to the radioman, his voice terse. "Call the general. Tell him we need two more artillery units and four more rifle units, or the right flank falls." The colonel refused to give up, even though he knew reinforcements would never come. General Javier Luis Américo was inexperienced and, in de Silva's view, an incompetent fool.

De Silva and Fifth Company were on their own. After spending many years in this godforsaken country and fighting in countless battles, he knew this situation would be the death of them all. But he had to try something.

"To the map . . . hurry!"

De Silva's officers gathered around as his calloused finger traced their precarious position on the map. "UNITA controls the high ground to our east, the rocky outcrops here." He pointed to the enemy UNITA's yellow pins on the map. "They are pushing us back, with First and Third rifles failing. This is driving a wedge between us and the main MPLA force. We're about to be cut off completely. With the river behind us, unless we make a move, we'll be surrounded and wiped out." His words hung in the tense air.

Although he looked cool and in control, de Silva's insides roiled with the dread of losing all his men. "Gentlemen, we are the point of the spear for Cuba and the MPLA. We cannot and will not fail Fidel or our country. *This*!" He hammered the map with the flat of his hand. "This is our duty and our life."

General Américo was in charge of the overall MPLA operation, and de Silva cursed him silently as he listened intently to the surrounding war. This chosen area was undefendable and there was no option to maneuver or strategically retreat. De Silva thought of *The Art of War* and Sun Tzu's instruction, "He will win who knows when to fight and when not to fight." He did not want to fight from this position, but General Américo was not a man to brook discussion or seek input.

Major Perez held his gaze in silent understanding. He and the colonel were close as brothers. Perez, having been trained by de Silva, had fought at his side for many years. The major's look said it all. They both knew this was likely the end.

A muscle ticked in the colonel's clenched jaw as unbidden memories resurfaced. His wife Maria Teresa's luminous smile. His little butterfly, Mariposa, growing up fatherless in distant Cuba.

De Silva realized again the enormous cost to his dedication. He had not seen Cuba or Maria in years. His daughter was growing up without her father. There had been years of bullets and dirt, and sun-drenched battles. Years of career successes and family neglect. His priorities had been wrong, and he felt the weight of guilt descend on his shoulders. His mind snapped back to the present as the sound of the battle roared back into his ears. UNITA forces were on the cliffs above their position.

De Silva felt a suicidal plan forming in his mind. A crazy last resort, a "Charge of the Light Brigade" type of plan, but one which no one would ever remember. He would marshal all of his forces, abandon their position, and attack the UNITA brigade to the west, where they were dug in and waiting. With a miracle, they could drive through the machine guns and mines, and reunite with the main force. This would make General Américo furious, but it might save about half of de Silva's men if they planned and executed correctly.

The Cuban colonel swallowed hard and stood straight. "Listen closely, comrades. We are going to—"

A deafening blast shattered the moment. The UNITA howitzer shell slammed into the northeast corner of the command tent like a thunderbolt straight from hell. The forty-four-kilogram fragmentation shell impacted the ground at six hundred meters per second with a violent impact of shockwaves and chaos.

Suddenly, de Silva was launched into the air, the world spinning in a chaotic blur of dust and debris. *This actually wasn't so bad*, he thought, *a slow-motion roller-coaster ride through space*. The ride over, he landed with a thud and rolled several times, dirt covering his uniform and rising in great puffs, rocks scraping elbows and knees.

He lay there; ears stopped working, stunned and motionless. De Silva gasped deeply, realizing he hadn't been breathing. The world began to speed up, and he took in his surroundings. Like a television on mute, there were no sounds, but he could see plenty of combat and fighting.

Perez lay motionless some ten meters away. De Silva staggered upright and lurched toward him, his Colt .45 coming automatically to his hand. His ears heard nothing, but he saw bullets kicking up geysers of dirt around them.

To his left, he could see two UNITA soldiers running up the hill toward their position firing AK-47's. One soldier had a camouflaged shirt with ragged shorts and flip-flops. His face was twisted in rage and terror, mouth open wide and teeth visible. The other soldier wore a fatigue cap and was bare-chested and barefooted.

De Silva's .45 barked, dropping the first man. He took two more steps forward when a bullet smashed into his left thigh. He steadied the .45 and crouched, aiming carefully despite his wound. His bullet sailed into the second man. De Silva moved forward, running in a shambling fashion and half dragging his left leg behind him. He had made it to the major.

De Silva crouched beside the major and felt for a heartbeat, two fingers on the carotid artery. No pulse. Perez's silver crucifix lay between them, stained with blood. The colonel placed a hand lightly on his friend's shoulder, saying goodbye, and closed his hand around the crucifix.

There were still no sounds in his ears, but the blossoms of dirt erupting were even closer now. De Silva crouched below the body, using it for cover as he raised his walkie-talkie and requested an urgent priority one helicopter evac.

Memories flickered behind de Silva's eyes—Maria Teresa's face on their wedding day in Santo Domingo. A welcome image of his butterfly, Mariposa, her delighted laugh as he tossed her playfully high in the air. Squeezing the crucifix tightly, he stood and snapped off three more shots, emptying his pistol before crouching again.

His thoughts turned to a secret location where a vast fortune in Angolan diamonds waited. Sparkling and glittering, they lay hidden, his legacy, waiting for someone brave enough to claim them.

CHAPTER 2
THE BUTTERFLY'S BOY

Altadena, California, October 26, 2009

Twenty-five years later, Colonel de Silva's namesake grandson, Mateus, threw himself sideways, the fragmentation grenade exploding in a searing blast. Shrapnel whipped through the air, fiery yellow sparks dancing across his vision.

Mateus rolled and fired his RPG in one fluid motion, the rocket's fiery exhaust scouring his face as it obliterated a cluster of twelve enemies to his right. He somersaulted and threw two quick grenades in succession, ten more bodies rag-dolling lifelessly through the air.

He surged forward only to be stopped by an incoming mortar exploding mere feet in front of him, the shockwave almost knocking him off his feet. Bullets stitched the air in angry streaks, coming from every direction. He was hit!

Mateus's body jerked from multiple bullet hits, his lifeless body crumpled in the dirt. The screen faded to black, and *GAME OVER* flashed repeatedly in the middle of the display.

"Crap," he said and turned to his high-powered desktop computer. Time to code. Fingers flew as he entered lines of the C programming language, integrating a new 3-D graphics engine into his video game.

One part of his mind was on the code, while the other was firmly in the 1775 Battle of Lexington. He could almost smell the acrid smoke, see the carnage, and hear the minieballs whine through the morning air. The blood-soaked Massachusetts countryside was strewn with 350 dead. His new Revolutionary War video game held promise if he could nail the authenticity and playability balance.

The bowl of ice chips on the cluttered Ikea desk table was mostly water. Mateus popped one of the remaining chips into his mouth and crunched absentmindedly, fingers still flying. A part of his brain thought for the thousandth time *nine-point-eight out of ten dentists recommend against eating ice chips*. But he munched another one anyway. There was also no doubt what the doctors would say about the vial of white powder sitting innocently next to the ice chips, seeming to vibrate seductively, a siren song whispering insistently for attention. Maybe he would take a hit for an energy boost before he studied. Mateus looked up from the vial to survey his apartment.

The dim, cave-like studio apartment was in Altadena, small and utilitarian. This was all he could afford on the doctoral fellowship from Cal Tech, the California Institute of Technology. The living room, dining room and bedroom were one and the same, with a bathroom and small kitchen off to one side. In a puzzling architectural choice, the few windows in the apartment were small and recessed, which let in almost no light. His standard joke to his best friend, Tay, was, "It may be small, but it's dark!"

The apartment had a large bookcase on one wall. A curious mix of highly academic textbooks, Tolkien hobbit tomes, biographies, Irish crime noir thrillers, and more filled the bookcase. His bed comprised a fold-out couch, which was adorned with blankets and an assortment of colorful pillows. His Ikea computer workspace sported two large screens and had both a powerful desktop computer and a beat-up looking gaming laptop. There was a worn dark Persian rug with hypnotic Arabic calligraphy decorating the center of the room.

Mateus took his ice chip bowl to the kitchen for a refill. The kitchen was simple but tidy, utilitarian. There was one high-tech corner that seemed out of place, something like John Travolta opening the briefcase in *Pulp Fiction*. Glowing and golden sat a De'Longhi Dinamica he used to make flawless cups of smooth Jamaican Blue Mountain coffee, espresso, cappuccino, and lattes. Its conical burr grinder provided fine, even grounds that left the rich flavor no place to hide.

It was coffee time. Healthier than the white powder going up his nose, it would do the job tonight for an energy jolt. His fingers flew nimbly across the De'Longhi, dials spun into precise positions. He started by adding cardamom and cocoa. Coconut sugar followed, made from the coconut palm tree sap of flower buds. He carefully measured each ingredient with a digital counter scale. A dash of cayenne completed the blend. With the four ingredients, he called this his C-4 biquadrate, or simply his *C-4 coffee*.

The kitchen filled with the rich aroma of java as his cell phone rang, revealing the smiling face of Tay, his best friend, on the screen. It was almost 2 a.m., but Mateus knew Tay would be up. Mateus and Tay grew up together and was his only friend, along with Muni, their female colleague computer scientist. Tay was a fellow Cal Tech student, fellow video gamer, and fellow genius.

"Tay, what's crakalackin?" Mateus said into the phone, a smile tugging at the corners of his mouth. Tay's upbeat energy never failed to lift his spirits.

"What's up buddy!"

"Just got wrecked on level 47 of *Lost Horizon*. Time for a little Revolutionary War game coding, and then I gotta study. You know how it is."

"Way too aggressive, man! Those upper levels take care and strategy, dude. I told ya a million times. Lay low and wait for your opportunities."

"Where's the fun in that?" Mateus laughed.

The two had bonded over video games and high-end scholastic achievement. The two smartest guys in their high school were together again at university. Tay always brought a smile to Mateus and a calmness to his spirit. He was the closest thing to family that Mateus had.

"Speaking of opportunity, Saturday night is Muni's costume party. And her birthday. There will be girl species there. I'll swing by and pick you up," said Tay. He knew that picking Mateus up was the only guarantee that he would show.

Mateus suppressed a groan. An introvert and borderline recluse, being roped into Muni's social gatherings always triggered anxiety. But Tay and Muni formed the whole of his human connections, as baffling as their insistence on parties and people might be. Muni's annual celebrations always drew in the eccentric intellects and kindred spirits who were more his speed.

With reluctance, Mateus replied, "Yeah, yeah. I guess," already dreading the event.

"What's your costume this time?" asked Tay.

"Schrödinger's Cat . . . um . . . again."

Tay laughed. "Yeah, man. Nothing screams fun and gets the ladies like a costume that includes a complex linear partial differential equation." His multi-colored dreadlocks shook with his amusement.

"What about you?" asked Mateus.

"I am going to wear my *dobok* robe and my black belt."

"Ha! Listen, karate kid. You're never going to get a girlfriend by showing off your nerd robe and dubious martial arts prowess," said Mateus.

"Well, you might be right if the last five years are any indication. See you on Saturday night."

"See you, buddy."

Mateus was back at the computer. He took a sip of the still hot C-4 coffee and absentmindedly fingered a worn jet-black rosary around his neck while cracking open a book. The title was *Theoretical Neuroscience / Computational and Mathematical Modeling of Neural Systems* by Laurence F. Abbott and Peter Dayan. He thought of his dissertation on neural networks and computational neuroscience. Mateus wanted to bridge the gap between human and complex machine interaction. Perhaps an artificial intelligence could one day seamlessly interface with the human brain, the biophysical mechanisms applied directly to computer simulations. It could be breakthrough time for paralyzed people.

He read at an astonishing pace, flying through the dense technical pages. There was no note taking. This information, even the statistical and complex mathematics, stuck to his brain like glue, automatically going into folders ready for later retrieval. It would be there waiting if he ever needed it. Tay and Muni called him "the computer" for good reason.

As he read, Mateus felt the familiar tug in his gut about his path. He saw his career laid out before him as clear as a New Mexico morning sky. *Finish PhD dissertation, become a professor at university, do about thirty-five years of research and teaching, retire, and likely die alone.* How lonely and uninspiring all of this seemed. No family, no wife, not even a girlfriend. His shyness and loneliness seemed lifelong and akin to a terminal sentence.

His gaze drifted to the lovingly assembled altar in the corner, illuminated by flickering candles. Mateus glanced there for comfort. It held the altar to his mom, Mariposa, the butterfly. A black-and-white photograph of her was in the center of the altar. Unsmiling, almost sullen, she had stared into the camera. Dark and stormy eyes like his own looked back at him.

She was tall and thin, maybe fifteen years old at the time, with clear light complexioned skin and curly black hair. For Mateus, it was like looking at a female version of himself, with an added set of dark bushy eyebrows. His thin six-two frame sat and watched her. Who was she, really? How had she died, so many years ago?

There were candles of varying sizes and shapes around the framed picture. They flickered and illuminated a rosary, a plate with three coins in it, a small white Buddha, and a picture of Jimmy Carter, the hero of the initial Cuban immigration to the US. The altar also held shells and a small bell in deference to the Santería religion.

A bust of Jesus with thorns on his head and the insignia *El Cristo de Olimpia* completed the altar. The bust had a secret—a hidden compartment in its bottom. Inside were several vials of white powder, lab-synthesized cocaine that Mateus believed he needed to function, his stash. He fingered the bust. Tempted.

Mateus had not really known his mother. An immigrant from Cuba, she had died in mysterious circumstances when he was only three years old. He had gone to live with Nilda, an older female cousin, in Houston.

His cousin was not unkind, but she was certainly uncommunicative and unloving. She was a small, single woman, a house cleaner who worked long hours and came home exhausted six days a week. There were no hugs, kisses, or helicopter parenting in Mateus's life. With Nilda's busy schedule, he found himself alone most of the time, submerged in the poverty-stricken neighborhood of Sharpstown in Houston.

Back to reality as Mateus looked morosely at the altar, thinking about his mom, Mariposa, the butterfly, dead some twenty years ago. She stared back at him with dark sad eyes, from a bleak black-and-white landscape. He reached into the statue for the vial of cocaine.

CHAPTER 3
MEETING FIDEL

Santo Domingo, Cuba, December 15, 1956

Almost thirty years before a howitzer blew him up, a young Juan de Silva gripped the cracked steering wheel of the beat-up truck and drove up the rugged switchbacks of Cuba's Sierra Maestra Mountain. Towering emerald pine trees and dense ferns moved slowly by. The springs groaned on the truck's bench seat as he wrestled with the balky manual steering, his thin arms straining.

Recruited by a friend to be a *campesino*, a supplies runner for Fidel Castro, de Silva felt a surge of pride as he ascended the mountain roads. He had recently learned to drive and was ready to help the cause. It was also a welcome respite from his life on the sugar plantation. His father, Martin de Silva, was the sugar plantation farm manager, a father who was mostly absent, a ghost who disappeared. Out of the house each day before dawn and working past sundown, always a stranger. De Silva had learned the meaning of duty from his father and not much else. Family was always a distant second to plantation needs.

Finally, de Silva navigated the last turn and made it safely to *Comandancia La Plata*, the guerrillas' mountain stronghold sitting high on the dusty plateau. He felt a bit nervous, remembering that just a few weeks ago, *The Granma*, a small vessel carrying Castro's tiny forces, ran aground in a mangrove swamp at *Playa Las Coloradas*. He had heard that Fidel was under fire from President Batista's troops and fled to the mountains to escape. Only nineteen half-drowned and bedraggled revolutionaries had made it to these mountains. These nineteen men needed supplies, and he was the *campesino* to make it happen today.

De Silva unloaded crates of precious medicine, fresh produce, and hearty loaves of bread from Santo Domingo into a tattered supply tent. His rubber-tire sandals carried him toward the command post. The nervous youth's pace slowed as raucous laughter echoed from within the army-green canvas walls. He gulped and walked inside, not knowing that the next few minutes would alter the course of his life.

Fidel's bark of a laugh echoed off the canvas walls, his mouth wide in an uninhibited grin. Companions, including Camilo Cienfuegos and the fiery Celia Sanchez, shared the laugh. But de Silva's gaze was on the charismatic Castro, seeing him wearing a very ordinary uniform of olive-green military fatigues, with pants tucked neatly into polished black boots. The trademark green jump-up hat was on the leader's head, a scoped rifle at his side. Castro's thick mustache and bushy mutton chop sideburns framed his face, below penetrating eyes that twinkled as he laughed.

De Silva cleared his throat and spoke, heart pounding. "*Comandante*, the supplies are . . . um . . . here, sir." He was not sure about this but on impulse gave a salute, right hand moving uncertainly to his temple, cheeks flushing. The tent fell silent. Fidel stopped laughing, rose to his full height, and crisply returned the salute.

The tent flap opened, interrupting the moment, and Ernesto 'Ché' Guevara, with his trademark beret tilted to the left, strode into the room. The Argentine revolutionary looked dubiously at de Silva, taking in his makeshift sandals, ripped shorts, sweat-soaked T-shirt, and tattered straw hat sitting atop his boyish features.

Ché burst into mocking laughter and said, "These soldiers of the revolution are getting younger and younger. This *pendeho* should still be suckling at his mother's teat."

Fidel frowned and started, "Ché, stop. This *campesino* is—"

"*Mi comandante*, with all respect," De Silva interrupted, straightening. "I don't need you to fight my battles." His gaze turned to Ché, unexpected steel in his youthful eyes. "I'm young. I don't have any money. But I believe in the revolution, and I am doing my part. Instead of thanks, you criticize. You should apologize to me. If this does not work for you, we can go outside, and I will teach you some respect."

The challenge hung in the air, a palpable tension. Ché took a tentative step toward de Silva.

"No, Ché," said Fidel.

Castro walked to de Silva, looked directly into his eyes, and put both hands firmly on the young man's shoulders. "You are the heart of the revolution. You have exactly what we need. Passion. Commitment. Sacrifice. Tell me your name."

"My name is Juan Antonio Mateus de Silva. I am the son of a sugar plantation farmer, and I have lived in Santo Domingo my whole life."

Castro's face lit into a wide smile. "They make them strong in Santo Domingo. Let's toast to Juan de Silva, raise a glass to the heart of our revolution!" He looked pointedly at Ché as he spoke and handed the boy a glass. They all drank, and the tent erupted in cheers.

After the burn settled down in his throat, De Silva said, "*Gracias mi comandante*. I am loyal and will gladly give my life to the cause." This brought claps to his back and another round of rum. Thoughtfully, de Silva walked directly to Ché and stuck out his hand. For a tense moment, the Argentine stared at the proffered hand. Then, finally, he clasped it in a grudging shake.

The trip back to Santo Domingo passed in a contented daze for young Juan de Silva, buzzed as much on the intoxicating experience as the rum's lingering warmth. Although it was late and fatigue tugged at his bones—his father would rouse him at 5 a.m.—he stopped by his girlfriend's house. Maria Teresa would be so excited to hear all the news. He was with Fidel!

When he got home and washed his face, he looked carefully in the mirror and smiled, the beaming glow of a newly made revolutionary. Tomorrow he would start to grow his mustache. He would wear it for the rest of his life.

CHAPTER 4
BIG MAN ON CAMPUS

Altadena, California, October 27, 2009

"Crap." Mateus muttered under his breath, his heart racing as he checked the time. He was dangerously close to being late for his morning class at Cal Tech. Not that it really mattered; he'd mastered the curriculum weeks ago. He'd not slept in forty-eight hours but felt awake and energized. The cocaine hit made his body feel alive and his mind euphoric. Mateus felt like he could conquer anything.

With practiced precision, he quickly brushed a small pile of the crystalline powder into a small vial and stashed it inside the hollowed base of his altar's Jesus bust. Taking one last swig of lukewarm coffee, he flew out the door, heading toward the bus stop and Cal Tech.

Backpack over one shoulder, the beautiful, stately old buildings of Cal Tech's buzzing campus passed in a caffeine-and-cocaine blur as Mateus made his way to the Computer and Neural Systems 487 class. A remarkable school for sure, but this was not a class he was looking forward to. He slipped quietly into the back row, his mind consumed with thoughts of his doctorate dissertation.

Cal Tech, on 124 acres in Pasadena, California, was one of the premier science and engineering schools in the world with some of the highest admission standards in the country. Even in the rarefied air of Cal Tech intellectuals, Mateus stood out. He devoured books and entire semesters of classes in short order. His photographic memory meant he did not take notes, and almost never missed a question on exams in any class.

Dr. Oliver Starkey, his PhD adviser, taught the 487 class. Mateus sat in the back, somewhat away from the other students, deep in dissertation thoughts.

"Mateus, if we take a standard analog silicone electronic circuit, how can the structure of this be made to be more neuron-like?" Starkey asked, intending to get Mateus's attention. "What is our vision here as we think about the relationship between the human body and advanced circuitry?"

Mateus's heart jumped to his throat as he woke from his reverie. He sighed inwardly and stood formally to answer the question, a quirk of his that drew rolled eyes from classmates. He nervously gulped, his mouth opening and closing as he hesitated and started to sit back down, then gulped again. The cocaine was wearing off, and with it, his confidence. How was he going to do this teaching stuff as a profession?

"Mateus, try again," said Starkey.

Mateus stood up straight, palms moist and sweat staining the armpits of his classic *Battle Gods* video game T-shirt. His bushy eyebrows rose as he stammered. "As we know, the full vertebrate nervous system contains both central and peripheral nervous systems . . ."

A long pause as he warmed up, mental circuitry starting to click. "Let's focus on the central system comprising the brain, retina, and spinal cord. Now imagine circuitry is used to improve or repair the connection between these systems." He was in a flow, nervousness lessening, emphatic gestures punctuating the air. "This circuitry also connects with the peripheral nervous system. If we could overlay the biological system with semiconductor backplanes, the computational . . ."

It went on like this for some time, with Dr. Starkey smiling knowingly at the front of class and his classmates taking furious notes.

Although brilliant, Mateus was shy and awkward at the best of times. This question was super easy though, at least for him, a fat pitch over the center of the plate. Mateus was working in this area in his PhD research, and it did him good to interact with classmates and prepare to be in front of the class himself in a few years.

"Great answer, Mateus. Thank you. I would like to have a quick meeting with you after class at The Broad."

The pair made their way in comfortable silence to The Broad Café, an on-campus coffee shop that they both favored. They sat, coffees in hand, relaxed after the short walk in the cool fall air. Mateus took out a small Ziploc bag with what was a precise mixture of his C-4 powder. He poured it deliberately into the coffee, staring intently at it dissolving as he slowly stirred. Mateus clearly liked his coffee and was particular about these additions.

"Are we boring you in this class?" Starkey asked.

"Little bit," said Mateus, giving a self-deprecating grin. "I know this stuff already."

"Well, get used to it. You'll be teaching this class before long, so it's important that you continue to grow in the classroom environment." Starkey's eyes were intense, a mixture of warmth and concern. "How's your dissertation coming along? It's important work. Your work could literally change lives for people afflicted with neural trauma and damage." Pride bloomed across the professor's features. "I'm damned proud of you, son."

Starkey paused, leaning back in his chair, shifting gears to the uncomfortable personal. "What are your holiday plans? Any Thanksgiving plans?" Starkey knew Mateus had no family in the Altadena area where he lived, or anywhere else.

"I may go over to Tay's house–err–Altheas's. No need to worry about this stray dog."

But Starkey's troubled frown remained, obviously noting the pallid complexion, feverishly dilated pupils, and disheveled hair. "You're looking a bit rough today. Everything alright?"

Mateus muttered, "Serotonin agonizes the 5-HT2A receptors in the brain, leading to dilation." Then louder, "I'm fine." With forced cheer, he drained his coffee, and the two men said their goodbyes. The professor was heading to give a lunchtime talk on Field Marshall Rommel's tactical brilliance, a special interest of his. Mateus just needed a nap.

Late that night, Mateus looked at the old blinking analog clock as he worked in an old basement campus lab, donated by Carl and Winifred Braun. His face scrunched in concentration as he stood over the lab bench, one of twelve in the room. For Mateus, this lab had the advantage of being deserted late at night, providing him with a place to synthesize his cocaine.

The 2:30 a.m. moon and stars shone into the room, illuminating his face as he bent over his work. Over the past two years, he refined his recipe, yielding a lab pure $C_{17}H_{21}NO_4$ synthesis that was fluffy and white and, to his mind, perfect. He was no addict, he figured, just an advanced individual who sometimes needed extra focus and extra nighttime study hours. And honestly, sometimes he enjoyed feeling like a superhero. He did not smoke or shoot up, restricting himself to snorting his own product and occasionally rubbing it on his gums.

Coca leaves were not the starting point for his formulation. Not only were they illegal in import into the United States, but it took bales of the stuff, hundreds of pounds, to produce any volume at all. Mateus did not need high volume, but just enough for his own personal supply. It was a point of pride for him that, although he was poor, he was no drug dealer.

Smiling as he bent over the iridescent ruby-red parr hydrogenation flask, he carefully added and stirred tropinone, ethanol, and sodium hydroxide. Complex and precise mixing. Hydrogen filtered nickel compounds, and pressurization. The resulting methylecgonine was of the purest order and the precursor to the cocaine. Adding it to a benzoic anhydride with a reflux step, hydrochloric acidification, ice bath cooling, and vacuum evaporation yielded the beautiful red oil. Mateus marveled every time at its brilliance and sparkle. His rocket fuel.

Mateus scooped the red oil into a special stainless-steel vial for transport. No reason to be walking around with cocaine in his pocket. With the cool night breeze on his face, he made his way to the shabby apartment for the simple final step, the addition of a touch of isopropanol. By dawn's light, he'd have the wonderful snow and be soaring high into the clouds.

CHAPTER 5
KILLING GROUND

Huíla Province, Angola, December 5, 1983

Three months before a howitzer detonated in his command tent, Colonel Juan Mateus de Silva surveyed the beautiful Tundavala Gap, just outside the city of Lubango. Emerald peaks and valleys unfurled in every direction, the crisp mountain breezes of the Huíla Province carrying whispered echoes of his Cuban hometown, Santo Domingo.

The colonel savored a rare moment of tranquility while sipping his fine coffee, one of his few vices, and breathed deeply the cool mountain air. Tundavala Gap might resemble paradise, but it was not a place to be visiting today; Colonel de Silva planned to use it as his killing ground. Even in the tranquility he could feel the weight of command squarely in his gut; people would die today.

De Silva's agile mind whirred, reviewing the tactical tomes lying in his tent—Sun Tzu's *The Art of War*, *On War* by Carl von Clausewitz, and other timeless works. De Silva, raised a conforming Catholic, still attended cathedral and confession when his duties allowed. But it was Sun Tzu and like-minded military strategists who he trusted and studied religiously.

The colonel had been fighting here for eight years. Cuba had been involved in Angola's brutal civil war since 1975, supporting the Soviet-backed Popular Movement for the Liberation of Angola (MPLA) against the US-backed National Union for the Total Independence of Angola (UNITA) rebels. The conflict, a proxy battleground for the Cold War between Moscow and Washington, had ravaged the young nation. More than ten years of relentless fighting caused the deaths of hundreds of thousands of Angolans and forced four million to flee their homes.

De Silva eyed the nearby UNITA encampment through his binoculars, critical of their haphazard formation. Based on what he saw and his own scouts' surveillance, UNITA's commander was a disorganized and undisciplined amateur.

The scouts—his ghosts, his shadows, his edge—were no mere observers. The *Las Sombras* scout force was de Silva's innovation, one of his secrets to becoming the most successful colonel in Angola. Trained in Russia, these spectral assassins killed with cold precision—slitting sentries' throats and silently disposing of their bodies, making it look like desertion to spread unease through enemy ranks. No other Angolan battalion employed them so extensively or lethally.

De Silva started with fourteen Las Sombras, but now had only nine, losing some to the enemy and some to hidden mines. Angola was the most mined country in the world and the MPLA's daring recons were constantly imperiled. The sting of these losses stayed with him and helped to steel his resolve.

Las Sombras had spent the past week extensively scouting the UNITA forces, which did not seem to know that their enemy was here. De Silva had led multiple strategy meetings with his officers, seeking their input on the battle plan. His righthand man, Major Maceo Perez, frequently contributed, which opened the door for the other officers.

With the decisions made, de Silva led the men in the final battle plan briefing. "Now is the time." De Silva looked each man in the eye. "We win with our plan. We win with Las Sombras and Los Coyotes.

We win with each other."

Los Coyotes were another of de Silva's innovations, the fastest and most experienced of his troops. These tough men proudly sported a cigar smoking coyote patch on their chest emblazoned with their *Rapido sobre dos piernas* (Fastest on two legs) creed. They served as de Silva's shock troops, carrying out astonishing hit-and-run assaults.

It was just before dawn on December 7. The significance of the Pearl Harbor date was not lost on de Silva. The leaders of the Sombras and Coyotes were with him in the command tent. All understood his role, so a simple nod from de Silva and they were off. These two teams would frame the day's battle.

The Sombras slipped through the dusky gloom first, fading like the evening mist toward enemy sentries. Along with a razor-sharp knife, they carried silenced TT-30 semi-automatic pistols. The Tula Tokarev design required a time-consuming pumping action for each shot, but with the Sombras, a single shot was enough. They knew where the sentries would be, and these men would soon be dead.

Salvador Chavez, a seasoned Sombra, swiftly incapacitated the final sentry, expertly severing his carotid artery with a clean slice. He moved smoothly to the side, dodging the ensuing crimson spray. His tight smile lasted for only a few steps as he circled back to rejoin the main force. The scouts knew the layout of the camp but had missed a small minefield, and Salvador unknowingly walked right into the danger zone.

The anti-personnel mine detonated and then roared. An earsplitting blast. A hot burst of air. Shrapnel. The explosion blew off Salvador's legs and he cartwheeled sickeningly into the air.

The sound from the mine field alerted the enemy, causing de Silva's forces to lose the element of surprise. But despite the mine's explosion, the plan was underway. It was almost dawn and time for the Coyotes.

The Coyotes split into two forces, and in a precise coordinated pincer movement, attacked the UNITA camp simultaneously. Each of the two forces put on an earsplitting terrifying show, with forty men throwing hand grenades and using rattling bursts of their AK-47's fire. In the early dawn light, it seemed to the waking UNITA soldiers that all the battalions in Angola had suddenly descended on their position.

The chaos inside the UNITA camp was almost total. Half-dressed soldiers running in all directions. Fumbling hands grabbing weapons. Confusing orders shouted in Spanish and Portuguese. One wild haired man shooting in random directions at no one. Friendly fire caused the first casualties of the day.

Deep in silk sheets and a cushioned cot, *Generalissimo* Horátio Ilidio slept deeply, his gentle snores filling the tent. A luxurious purple satin sleeping mask covered the eyes of the strikingly handsome man against any stray campfire light.

The former UNITA explosives engineer had clawed his way to command through suicidal bravado and a ruthless string of victories. His rapid promotion was a part of the attempted "Angolization" of UNITA leadership, trying to get more Angolan nationals into leadership positions.

"*Generalissimo . . . señor*, wake up. Please, sir!" His aide was at the tent flap, not daring to stick his head inside, despite what was going on in the camp. Ilidio was pissed. It was still dark outside and earlier than he liked to rise. As he prepared a suitable rebuke for his aide, he heard the battle sounds. Without dressing, he ran to the command tent, sleeping mask fluttering to the ground and heart pumping.

Fidel's rebel scum sends yet another scouting patrol on my men? So be it. His eyes narrowed, hardening with resolve as he thought of past victories. *A small rebellion. Easy.* Ilidio shouted, "Launch an immediate full-scale counterattack! We will crush these *putas*!"

Adrenaline surged. This was his time. Another victory! A triumph so early in his generalship would impress the charismatic Jonas

Savimbi, head of UNITA forces, and Ilidio benefactor.

While General Ilidio had been at the knife-edge of many engagements in the past, he preferred to fight at a distance now. Still, he had the aide bring his Jeep around. He mused. Once these upstarts were defeated, he would ride to the front, congratulate his men, and bask in their adulation. An Angolan Caesar.

As the aide rushed away, he had another thought and shouted after him, "Be sure and bring the camera!" These pictures would go to Savimbi and to his dad. He would show them both.

The UNITA forces finally mobilized, their leaders getting the squads organized to form lines. As the lines formed, the battle shifted dramatically. When the Coyotes encountered these newly formed UNITA lines, they turned and ran, as if in fear. Every twenty steps, they would turn, fire a burst from their rifle, and continue on.

The UNITA forces followed, running en masse and excited to be winning this battle, which at first seemed so hopeless and chaotic. They were eager to put down this small patrol. Their leaders shouted, urging them forward with ever greater speed. Virtually every UNITA man had joined in the chase. The Coyotes converged at the entrance to a narrow gorge. Without a pause, they ran into the gorge at full speed, UNITA forces on their heels.

As the UNITA forces entered the gorge, they saw the Coyotes ahead. They gleefully charged as they seemed to have the small patrol cornered. From his position on the rim of the gorge, de Silva watched it all through his binoculars, lips pressing into a tight smile as his trap unfolded. The killing ground.

The top of the gorge had hundreds of concealed soldiers, most with AK-47 or AKM assault rifles. These well-disciplined de Silva troops remained hidden and had not fired a single shot. Machine-gun nests lay on both sides of the gorge, Soviet-made DShK, firing 12.7

mm rounds at a devastating high rate. The MPLA had carefully placed hidden C-4 charges at strategic points on the cliff faces, ready to blast the incoming enemy.

Most of the sizable UNITA force had entered the gorge when unexpected thundering noises from behind caught them off guard. From concealed locations, eight BTR-60 Armored Personnel Carriers (APCs) had started their engines and broken from cover. The machines, bristling with heavy machine guns, were ominously rolling toward the UNITA men.

Major Perez was in the lead APC, standing on top of it like some sort of Cuban General Patton, directing the charge. On his command, the APC's stopped. De Silva's soldiers poured out of the open top, firing as soon as they hit the ground. The 20 mm cannons on the APC started firing in unison.

The APC fire was devastating, and the UNITA forces sprang farther into the gorge to get away from it. They ran with desperation and fear, adrenaline pumping and reason leaving them. When they reached the designated point inside the gorge, de Silva's MPLA soldiers on the rim opened fire.

Back at their camp, two wily and battle-hardened UNITA sergeants had resisted the urge and disobeyed the order to pursue the intruders. They made their way to the UNITA artillery battery. A bank of three G5 South African towed howitzers sat at the ready. They put a shell into the breach of the first one and adjusted their firing coordinates toward the emerging APCs. A blasting whoosh and distinctive thunder marked the firing as the men covered their ears.

The shell landed on the right side of the third APC, mushrooming into a hell burst of shrapnel, lifting it into the air and turning it over. This instantly killed seven men with three more alive but trapped under the wreckage. Perez pivoted, ordering his two lagging APCs to charge the artillery battery. As they started to move, a second shell hit, wide this time but shaking the ground and deafening ear drums.

The ambush continued in the valley. Heavy machine guns and

assault rifles burst into life simultaneously. UNITA soldiers were mowed down in waves. The attackers hit the men from all directions. Right. Left. From behind. In a *coup de grâce*, they detonated the C-4 charges and put down anything left alive in the killing ground. The APCs made quick work of the sergeants at the artillery units, hitting them with bursts of machine-gun fire even as they frantically left the howitzer and scrambled for cover.

It was over in minutes. De Silva looked up at the sky with a grim smile. He raised a finger in thanks to the Holy Mother, as well as to Sun Tzu and Napoleon.

CHAPTER 6
A BIRTHDAY FOR MUNI

Pasadena, California, October 27, 2009

The throaty growl of the 327 V8 motor reverberated through the 1967 Mustang as the shiny maroon fastback coupe roared down California's 210 freeway. The speedometer's needle crept past seventy-five as Jay-Z's "Empire State of Mind" blared from the speakers. Tay's free hand unconsciously bobbed to the beat as the motor rumbled. A tall ex-basketball player, turned Ford maniac, had lovingly restored the Mustang in Somis, California.

"Whoa there, cowboy, let's not get a ticket here." Mateus de Silva gave a weak smile from the passenger seat.

Best friend Tay shot him a wolfish grin and pressed his foot down, shooting more gas into the Mustang's Autolite 2100 series carburetor. The dreadlocked young Tay came from money, his dad a cardiologist at a leading Houston Heart and Vascular Institute. This allowed for a nice wardrobe, some toys like the Mustang, and the occasional moving violation. Tonight though, it was Muni's birthday and Halloween party. They were running a bit late, providing a good excuse for the speed.

"So, Schrödinger's cat," Tay said, glancing sidelong at his friend's complicated costume, complete with a stuffed calico cat affixed to his shirt. "You realize that ninety-nine percent of the population won't get your little science getup, right?"

"It's a good thing she didn't invite the McDonald's and Walmart crowds tonight. Anyone on Muni's guest list will understand quantum mechanics and know that a cat can be simultaneously dead and alive. So, deal with it, bub."

"Great. I have an aggressively elitist feline for a best friend," Tay shot back with a laugh, merging lanes with a squeal of rubber.

The wind whipped through their hair as they rocketed down the freeway. Mateus always wrestled with his discomfort at social gatherings. The idea of opting out was tempting, but some excuse like "PhD research emergency" sounded lame even to him. His shyness at parties felt like a flashing light on top of his head screaming, "THIS GUY IS UNCOMFORTABLE!"

He would need a bump to get through this thing and patted his right leg to feel the comforting metal cylinder in the seam. One tiny bump would be all he needed to make it through the evening.

At least Tay will be there to run interference. Mateus smiled across at his friend, watching Tay's dreadlocks swirl, looking almost alive in the wind. *Still need that bump.*

The party was in full swing when they arrived, music and conversation swirling around them. They made their way to the living room, moving toward some familiar whoops of triumph. Muni, dressed as Gandalf, was using the controller to steer her Bowser character around a mine and over a tricky jump on the big-screen TV. She was in the lead with the Halo's Master Chief firing coconuts from his *Mario* car without effect.

"This race's mine, ya orcs!" Muni said, her dark eyes bright and twinkling behind the fake silver beard.

Muni's birthday party was off to a great start. Her two-bedroom apartment was spacious and easily accommodated eight guests. The music blared Japanese electronica, math rock, and inexplicably The Cowsills and The Monkees within the mix.

Mateus took in the Halloween-themed cake that was already

half eaten and looked like someone had accidentally stepped on one corner. He cataloged the costumes: a stoic Carl Sagan sipping a beer; a spot-on Marie Curie flirting with Halo's Master Chief; a Devo band member complete with a conical energy dome hat. These all seemed more impressive than his cat. As always, Mateus felt like he did not quite belong.

He had already managed to spill some cake on his chest, which had not improved his shaky confidence. His eyes missed little though, despite not engaging. Several people gathered around Tay, who was laughing in his martial arts uniform as he told a funny story about speeding through a Cal Tech parking lot. At least one of them could relax and let his guard down once in a while. Tay's magnetism and affability never ceased to amaze.

"I used my arm to cover my head so he couldn't see me. Like there are thirty or forty Black guys with classic Mustangs at Cal Tech." Tay smiled as the partygoers laughed.

Muni, even while driving the video game car, confidently spoke of an Indian IRS scam she had hacked into. Her voice rang out in the apartment.

"So, next I crashed their scamming Mumbai servers, deleted all their personal phone data, including pictures and contacts, and gave them personal financial and banking headaches that are gonna hurt for a while. Their next trip to the ATM or look at any online credit check, they are in for a big surprise!" The partygoers laughed appreciatively. "Hopefully, this encouragement gets them into a new line of work and protects some gullible old folks and their life savings."

Muni was a senior at Cal Tech, a computer science major. She had skills and was a "hacker for good" or ethical hacker in her spare time, destroying fake IRS call centers and scams that preyed on the uninformed or gullible. Loud but tender-hearted, her tough exterior had a sensitive inside once you got close. A second generation Korean American, her father and mother were both professional musicians, a cellist and flutist respectively, who played in symphony orchestras. In high school, her given musical name of Harmony was shortened to Muni, and the name stuck.

Tay looked over at Mateus and noticed he was not interacting much. Similar high school memories came back to him. They both had Advanced Placement (AP) physics in senior year, a tough class with only seven students and an engaging teacher named Mr. McDougle. The two young men ended up partnering on the class's special project. Tay learned that Mateus had read and absorbed the entire physics book during the first couple of weeks of class. Physics came easily to Mateus, and Tay knew he was exceptional, but not at that level.

Their physics project set a new standard for the school. It was called "The Frictionless Heavy Mover" and used advanced magnetics, a sophisticated numerical control system, and state-of-the-art materials technology. It had potential application for large warehouses and other industry. The instructor encouraged them to apply for a utility patent, which they did. The project bonded them, and they had been friends ever since.

At the party, Mateus said, "I'll be right back," excusing himself for the bathroom. Once inside, he carefully cleaned and dried Muni's handheld mirror, sprinkling a small amount of white powder on its surface. His formulation was so pure and snow-like that there was no real need to chop it with a razor blade. He sniffed quickly, once for each nostril, and checked carefully in the mirror for any telltale sign. Vial hidden back in his pant seam, he rejoined the party, blood roaring and confidence soaring.

Muni called out loudly, "Okay guys, time for some bridge!" Contract Bridge was their game, even for Mateus, who felt much less socially awkward while playing. The remaining partygoers were invited, at least in part, for their expertise in bridge. There were three from Cal Tech, one from UCLA, and finally Hugh, from the Sepulveda Best Buy Geek Squad.

Wigs and capes and masks came off, and the group settled in at the tables. Muni's spiky purple hair and piercings were visible without the hood, and she looked decidedly un-Gandalf-like. Her worn black Doc Martin lace-up boots were visible, with the robe off. She was striking and beautiful, with Tay and Mateus looking at her appreciatively, but their love was decidedly sisterly in nature.

Muni was an assertive host and set the bridge teams. From longstanding agreement, Tay and Mateus were not allowed to be partners. They seemed to share some sort of telepathic connection that the rest of the group put down to a kind of uncatchable cheating. Mateus pulled out a worn silver flask and set it next to the ice chip bowl Muni had put in front of him.

"My drinks not good enough?" asked Muni. This was a routine for them.

"Not unless you have eighteen-year-old Macallan single malt somewhere hidden in the cupboard," said Mateus.

"I wouldn't bring it out for you if I had it."

Mateus took a healthy swig from the flask, tasting the notes of ginger, dried fruit, and toffee. The whiskey burned slightly as it went down. The primary effect though, was that it increased the amount of cocaine in his bloodstream by over thirty percent. He felt the cocaine out to the tips of his fingers and toes. The whole-body experience was comforting, exhilarating, and confidence-building. *I'm going to win this bridge tourney and be social at the same time. Just watch.*

"Daydream Believer" was blaring on the stereo, and Mickey Dolenz' voice sounded as good as ever. Mateus took a piece of ice from his ice bowl and sipped appreciatively at his flask. He opened the bidding with four hearts, a very aggressive opening, holding the cards in an unsuccessful bid to hide the cake stain on his shirt. Muni responded with, "The Computer does not have two hearts, let alone four! He's a tin man. We all know that. Pass."

Mateus said quietly, "Balrog, you shall not pass."

Even with her Gandalf hat off to one side, Muni smiled. "That's my line and you know it!"

Mateus counted every card and was comfortably ahead when

his cell phone started buzzing in his pocket. Unknown number but overseas. *Hmm.* Over protestations from the table, he excused himself and went into one of the two bedrooms.

"Hello."

The voice responded, "*Hola. Este es Dolores Gomez.*"

"Sorry. I don't know you. You have the wrong number." His words were slightly slurred with cocaine and whiskey. He started to hang up.

"Wait. Wait. I am your aunt from Cuba and I need to—"

"I don't have any aunts. Goodbye." Mateus was through with this and ready to get back to bridge.

"Your *abuela, mi madre,* is dying!" Even from four thousand miles away, Mateus could hear that the voice was strained. The "*madre*" word caught his attention and his lightning-quick mind went to work, racing even in his dulled state. Her last name was Gomez, which was his grandmother's maiden name. An illegitimate daughter might take the mom's name for her own last name. The name Dolores fit as well, a first name meaning *sorrows.*

As the words ricocheted around his brain, Mateus thought about family. His mom was really his only family, and she was long gone, dying when he was three. His grandmother in Cuba wanted nothing to do with him. As a young boy, he had sent many letters to her without a reply. Mateus had written in pencil, using his best handwriting, but all in vain.

The letters included questions about his mother, his grandfather, and Cuba. Even at a young age, he knew enough not to ask about his father. He was eager to connect with her, but finally received a curt "quit bothering me" reply. As much as he pushed it deep down, this was a wound and something he didn't understand, then or now.

"I'm listening," he said.

"Your grandmother is dying in Santo Domingo." *My grandmother? Maria Teresa, the Cuban lady who wanted nothing to do with me?* His heart fluttered with emotion. While she had never liked him, she was still a relative and the only one he had. This was also the last tie to his grandfather and namesake, Juan Mateus de Silva, the colonel and war hero.

Dolores continued. "She is asking for you. You need to come here to Cuba, right now." Mateus felt shocked. Why reach out at the end, beg for his presence in her last moments? It didn't make any sense.

"What is she saying, exactly?"

Dolores paused then replied quietly. "*El bastardo. La caja de puros. El Bastardo.* She says this over and over."

No one had ever spoken to Mateus about his father. Even while it hurt, his analytical mind reckoned being called *"the bastard"* was probably accurate. Who was he really? *Caja de puros* meant cigar box. That was even more mysterious. He did not smoke and had never even had a cigar.

Dolores said curtly, "You need to come here. Now! *Andale.*" She hung up the phone.

Well, that's not going to happen. Mateus had a powerful fear of flying. He had never flown in his life and planned to never set foot on a plane. He knew all the statistics cold, to the third decimal, but that did not change his mind. Probably driving with Tay in his Mustang was way riskier than flying, but still.

He called Muni and Tay into the bedroom. "It's my grandmother in Cuba," he whispered at last, still reeling from the news. "She's d-d-dying. Asking for me to come there. To Santo Domingo." They knew his history and his preference to stay at home with his research.

Tay said, "This is your grandmother. Family. C'mon, buddy. You have to do this. Don't miss this."

Muni looked around the room, as if to make sure the FBI and the DEA were not eavesdropping. "Listen, my little bridge player, I have a friend in the chemistry department at Cal Tech. I'll get you some pills that make Valium seem like a placebo. You WILL be relaxed on that plane. Guaranteed." Mateus shook his head no, no, no as they continued to try to persuade him.

Mateus lay in his bed that night, tossing and turning. His fever dreams were all about Cuba. *I can't do this,* and *she never liked me anyway* battled with *only family I have* and *why was she talking about me and a cigar box?*

Upon waking, he carefully made the C-4 coffee, a typical start to the day. What followed was anything but typical. Almost without thinking, he packed a small bag and took a taxi to the airport. His brain was on autopilot. No thought, just action. If he stopped to think, he would go back to the stable path of school and study. He even left without cocaine for fear of discovery and arrest.

Muni met him at the airport with a small, unmarked bottle of pills. "Two every twelve hours, Matty, no more!"

Mateus sat cramped in his economy seat, not built for his long legs, and popped two of the pills. He stared at a third pill with some longing but thought better of taking it.

He fingered the jet-black rosary around his neck and thought about Cuba and the grandmother he had never met.

CHAPTER 7
THE FUNERAL

Santo Domingo, Cuba, October 30, 2009

Muni's miracle pills worked wonders; Mateus made it to Santo Domingo with no plane crashes or terrorist hijacking panics. His Aunt Dolores hustled him through the small home's musty interior and into a dimly lit back bedroom. There, for the first time, he saw Maria Teresa, his grandmother on her death bed.

She was just a wisp of a person beneath the coarse sheets. Lying still. Eyes closed. Translucent pale skin. Frail. Still, he could see himself as an echo of this lady, seemingly barely alive. Mateus struggled to breathe and tried to smother unfamiliar emotions that welled up in his heart.

"Grandmother? *Abuela*?" he whispered, as if afraid louder words might hurt her.

Maria's eyes fluttered open with visible effort and she struggled to speak. "*Mijo*?" she asked, her reedy voice cracked like red sunbaked clay.

"Yes. I am here, *abuelita*." His heart clenched despite the decades of bitter disappointment at her indifference. Still, he reached for her parchment-thin hand, its web of distended purple veins and papery skin dry to the touch.

"*Mi Bastardo*," she whispered, a soft breathy hiss. "Get the cigar box, *los puros*."

"*Sí, mi abuelita.*" An unexpected grin tugged at Mateus's lips. Maria had acknowledged him as kin. He held onto her hand, cherishing the unaccustomed moments with family. But her eyes remained closed, and she stopped speaking. Forever. Maria Teresa de Silva slipped away quietly in the middle of that starless Cuban night.

The battered black hearse was old and listed to the right. Weathered paint. Mismatched tires and rims. The vinyl covering on the roof was peeling and red rust showed through. It was special and important in Mateus's eyes as it held the remains of his grandmother.

The hearse moved slowly down the streets of Santo Domingo. Following were Mateus, his Aunt Dolores, and a few older friends of Maria Teresa's. The people walked wearily, heads down, toward the cemetery.

Maria Teresa never remarried after the death of her husband, Juan Mateus de Silva, in Angola. She had lived in the same small house since her wedding in 1965. The town, her house, and her few friends. This was her life. Mateus, the only child of Mariposa, was her descendant and she had never wanted to have anything to do with him.

The cheerless procession slowly passed the weather-beaten adobe homes and small shops of Santo Domingo before stopping at the Gothic coral tinted limestone walls of *Catedral de Santa Maria la Menor*. Completed in 1541, it was the oldest cathedral still standing in the Americas, its scuffed walls radiating centuries of forgotten secrets.

As was common, the tired, red-eyed priest had not been informed of the funeral. He had grown accustomed to these instantaneous ceremonies. After a curt nod at his parishioners, he performed the last sacrament in less than five minutes, the words tumbling out in well-rehearsed Latin.

Mateus heard the Latin and translated automatically in his mind. "*Through this holy anointing, may the Lord in his love and mercy help you with the grace of the Holy Spirit."* The priest droned, syllables slurring against one another in his haste. *"May the Lord, who frees you from sin, save you and raise you up."*

The procession thinned as the hearse drove toward its endpoint. At the small tidy cemetery, the flowers were transferred from the hearse to the graveside. The coffin lowered into the ground as the remaining six people bowed their heads in respect.

Along with this modest gathering, Santería offerings would come later. The Santería religion was strong in Cuba, with its West Africa roots and fusion with Roman Catholicism. Mateus knew that over the next year a Santería rite would also take place, the *levantamiento de platos* (breaking of the plates). This was supposed to help the soul in its journey to the afterlife.

Walking back to his grandmother's house after the funeral, Mateus pondered about family and the enigmatic remarks regarding a cigar box. The reddish dust from the road swirled around his legs as the setting sun radiated a beautiful technicolor display of purple and orange. Both the funeral service and sunset held the essence of Cuba, evoking a sense of family. Family was pain. An ache. A hole in his center.

Images of last Thanksgiving rose unbidden. Mateus had been the special guest of Tay's warm family. It took a lot of arm-twisting by Tay, and even a few arguments between them. In the end he showed up, feeling awkward and shy.

Tay and his two brothers had sat with their dad, watching the Dallas Cowboys and Oakland Raiders on television. This was a Raiders' household with jerseys and merch; even Tay's mom donned Raider's logo pirate earrings. Mateus was not a sports guy, and could not really join in. Shyness and lack of knowledge left him sitting silently, off to the side and away from the action.

There was shouting and back-slapping at the good plays, and moans of disgust at fumbles or missed tackles. The coach's intelligence and ancestry were questioned as the Cowboys looked to be pulling away for the win. Mateus finally made his way to the kitchen where

Tay's mom was cooking. She made him comfortable, and before long, he found a role as the head gravy stirrer.

Tay's dad, Altheas, carved the turkey, confidently making long slices. As he cut, he gave a lecture on turkey carving and how to improve his Raiders. Somehow, he cleverly wove these two topics together. Although not a big man, to Mateus he seemed huge and in control. The love of family was palpable. Mateus could reach out and touch it . . . smell it . . . feel it.

The dinner was wonderful, the food delicious, but Mateus ate little and tasted less. Instead, he was soaking in this family's interactions, somewhat in awe. The family joked and lovingly teased one another. Tay's mom kept order and was positive, building everyone back up. They were purposeful in making Mateus feel included. Wonderful.

I've never had this. I never will have this. No girl, no prospects, not even a social life to speak of. My work and career are not a substitute for family, Mateus self-admonished.

Blinking away the melancholy reverie, he was back at his grandmother's humble home, the small funeral troupe sitting and quietly reflecting on her life. Not comfortable and an outsider, with no stories to add, Mateus sat awkwardly off to one side. His right leg bounced like a small rotary engine, the wooden chair beneath him creaking in time.

Despite all this, he was alert and listened carefully to every word. Maria Teresa had clearly been a woman of dignity and pride. She was a woman of sorrow. Losing her husband and then her daughter left her alone with her grief. She had never stopped loving her husband, and she organized several masses in his honor at the cathedral. The shadowy circumstances around his Aunt Dolores' conception remained unmentioned.

His body felt the cravings as his leg kept jack hammering anxiously.

He longed for the fiery euphoria of a modest pick-me-up bump. Why hadn't he smuggled his stash onto the flight? The mourners ate a light dinner together and spoke more of Maria Teresa, anecdotes and stories. Gradually, the people said their hushed farewells and left, leaving Mateus alone with his mysterious aunt.

"Who are you? Why were you a secret to me?"

Dolores paused and stiffened, eyes hooded and plump lips tightening into a thin line. "My father was a local Communist party official. Umm. He had another wife and family and . . . well something went down one night with your *abuela*, ya know, and I was the unexpected result."

A long pause and then Mateus said quietly. "So, while she dismissed me as her bastard grandson, you lived under her roof your whole life as a daughter? That makes no sense." Mateus shook his head in disgust and confusion.

"Don't be too hard on your grandmother. She never could accept you because of how you were conceived. But I was here with her. Born of her flesh and blood, and I was all she had."

"And my grandfather?" Mateus persisted. "Colonel Juan Mateus de Silva himself? He was always my hero. He knew Fidel Castro and Ché and went to Africa to fight for Cuba. I was named after him. Did he know about you?"

She nodded. "He always believed it was rape. Unforgiveable. A death sentence if the colonel would have gotten to my biological father. He never stopped loving Maria Teresa, but it changed him, and broke something inside your *abuelo*. I could see from the letters. His rosy-eyed view of communism and duty was gone. Made him bitter, and angry."

Mateus sat back and ran his hand through thick, curly black hair. "Then what's this nonsense about a cigar box? I don't understand. Some final test from my grandmother?"

With a wordless beckoning gesture, Dolores motioned for him to follow and grabbed a small ladder from a kitchen corner. Dolores took the ladder to an attic entry in the ceiling of the small bedroom closet.

Leaning the ladder against the opening and climbing, she motioned for Mateus to follow.

They climbed in silence, Mateus stopping and then letting his eyes adjust to the gloomy space. Shadowed trunks. Old broken furniture. Stacks of newspapers and magazines. And a single large hope chest, wisps of cobwebs trailing from its lid.

"These were your grandfather's belongings," she explained, as Mateus unbolted the rusty latch and opened the chest. A small cloud of dust rose as the lid creaked open, sending him into a fit of coughing.

No glowing treasure or gemstones here. Quite an ordinary find. Old pants and shirts. Cotton and linen fabric. An ancient pair of his grandfather's black wingtip shoes lay inside, which Mateus suspected were reserved for special occasions or church.

He lifted one of the shoes, marveling at how the buttery soft leather was so well preserved. Slipping his foot inside first one and then the other, the moment became magical. They fit as if custom made for his feet.

His bushy eyebrows went up in surprise even as a wash of affection hit him. This was a connection to his grandfather. His blue eyes began to water, a lonely tear rolling down his right cheek. Dolores put a comforting hand on his knee. He gave a shaky smile and removed the shoes.

Deeper into the chest, and even in the dim light, he saw a splash of color under an old shirt. Pushing aside the clothes, he discovered a colorful cigar box hiding beneath. He went back down with Dolores into the house, carrying the shoes and the box.

The cigar box was striking, with the top showing a beautiful lady in a formal dress. A bouquet of flowers was in one hand and a book in the other. She looked happy and content. Above her head were the word *Habana* and below her *La Exportadora*. The color and detail were exceptional and spoke of another time.

Mateus opened the box and was surprised to still catch the faintest whiff of cigar despite its age. There was a sheaf of yellowed letters inside and a single black-and-white photo. Small, dried remnants of tobacco leaves sat forgotten in one corner of the box.

The vintage photo showed six Cuban soldiers, five holding AK-47's and wearing hats. They scowled fiercely at the camera. The sixth man was in the middle and hatless, clearly his grandfather.

This was the first picture of Colonel Mateus de Silva he had ever seen. He was cradling a small sub-machine gun and smiling, the thick black hair and bushy eyebrows achingly reminiscent of Mateus's own. On the back of the picture, the faded scrawl said simply, *Juan, 8/29/81*.

Mateus tried to hand the cigar box back to Dolores, who simply shook her head no and pushed it back to him. In his room that night, he opened all the brittle envelopes containing his namesake's precise handwriting. All were routine except the one on top. This first letter spoke simply with eloquent Spanish words. Love. Future. Togetherness. It ended with a poem that to Mateus seemed strange. The Spanish did not flow, and the wording was off, the lyrics strange and haunting.

Our Marriage

Our marriage, like a beloved cathedral in the capital city
Our marriage, like a lady who is the remedy of my life
Look, look, to this cathedral for the prize
Look, look, for it is there waiting

This cathedral, the biggest and best around
This cathedral, not quite the oldest to be found, is our remedy
Look to the crypt, entombed and waiting to be found
The treasure, the future for our marriage, is;

> *buried beneath the watchful eyes of Jesus on the cross*
> *guarded by our mother Mary who stands in the light of day,*

Your Juan

The words swam in his vision as Mateus read and reread the enigmatic poem, not knowing it was something he would obsess over and words that would eventually lead him to Angola and on a perilous treasure hunt. He was hyper-focused on the sheet of paper and never once glanced out the window.

Across the street sat a dark man with unblinking eyes, watching Mateus intently. The man was used to waiting, after these many long years. He had picked up Mateus's trail at the funeral, using a cell phone with a spider's web of cracks on its screen to make an overseas call. Angola came on the line, and he couldn't wait to cash in on a long-awaited reward.

CHAPTER 8
LEAVING HOME

Santo Domingo, Cuba, September 12, 1980

Mateus and his Aunt Dolores sat at the worn wooden table eating breakfast, their relationship having softened with the shared funeral, cigar box opening, and the sunlight from a new day. The conversation was coming easier.

"My mother died when I was three. What do you know about her?"

"I know some of the story of your mother," Dolores said. "But it's not a happy tale."

"I need to hear it. All of it. Please, Dolores."

As she spoke, Dolores' sonorous voice lulled him, and he submerged into the story of his mom, Mariposa, the butterfly.

Mariposa Anrieth de Silva pushed the soggy scrambled eggs around her chipped plate, unable to take a single bite. Her eyes were red, and her hair was a mess. Mariposa felt scared. The muffled sobs of her mother, Maria Teresa, pierced the thin walls of their house, each cry of *"Marielitos. Marielitos,"* stabbing her heart like a knife.

Mariposa left the eggs, cold and uneaten, and stood to get her weathered bag. The fifteen-year-old girl prepared to leave her mom and younger stepsister to start a new life. Her father was dead, and this seemed the only way out of suffocating poverty.

They had agreed. Done. But sadness threatened to overwhelm her as this *Marielito* prepared to leave her home and her precious mom. The death of Mariposa's father Colonel de Silva in Angola had pulled them together in a bond born of grief, and leaving was breaking both of their hearts.

"Mama?"

Her mom, Maria Teresa, was on the couch, unable to speak. Mariposa drew a deep breath and knew she had to be the strong one here.

"Mama. I'm a *Marielito* now. The boat will take me from Port Mariel to Key West. You know this. Fidel has given his blessing and even President Carter has said, 'We welcome you with open arms.' This is the only way."

"It is too far, *mija*, too dangerous. I have a terrible feeling." Facts supported Maria Teresa's intuition. The eighty-seven-mile journey, sometimes in decrepit boats, would cause many Cubans to lose their life at sea, despite the best efforts of the US Coast Guard. Mariposa was joining 125,000 others, including inmates and political dissidents, all jumping into the treacherous Gulf of Mexico.

Mariposa wrapped her mom in a fierce embrace, memorizing her scent. Maria Teresa, unable to speak, made the sign of the cross and pressed a jet-black rosary into Mariposa's palm. With a last kiss on her mother's wet cheek, she stood and walked out the door.

The familiar streets of Santo Domingo passing under her feet, she made her way to cousin Nilda Ruiz's house, small dust clouds kicking up with every step. The two girls had been inseparable since birth, their bond closer than sisters. They sat in the same classes at school, with Nilda hardly ever speaking in class. They explored all the mountain trails around there, arm in arm. And now, they were crossing together.

Mariposa looked around Santo Domingo as she walked. One last time. To her right, she could observe the banks of the Rio Yara and the Sierra Maestra mountains towering behind them, a sight of breathtaking beauty and purity. She had hiked there often, even going past Fidel Castro's rebel hideout, *La Comandancia de la Plata*. She felt a familiar burst of pride in thinking of her father, Juan Mateus de Silva, who had helped to supply and protect this hideout.

Mariposa drew a deep breath to calm her nerves and to taste the fresh and crisp air. In the dirt front yard, Nilda had tied up her scruffy brown dog with an old rope. The dog knew Mariposa well, but still snarled and showed his yellowed teeth, straining against the rope, more as a matter of routine than true menace.

She waited for some time, sitting on the porch with the old dog, while Nilda finished saying her goodbyes. Finally, her aunt and Nilda were on the porch with her, tears in their eyes, sharing one last embrace. Her aunt wore a simple light brown dress, her hair pulled tight into a bun, a perpetual frown lining her face.

She hugged her aunt. "Thank you, *tia*, for paying for this. *Gracias*. I wish you and my mom were going with us."

A rare smile and a resigned shrug. "This trip took all the money. You two need a chance for a better life. Your mom and I will be okay here. It's all we've ever known, anyway."

Nilda's mother had used most of her life's savings for the crossing. No one in the family could imagine the two girls being separated and in different cities, let alone different countries. They were going together to the new world, leaving Santo Domingo forever.

Their goodbyes completed, the girls walked to the bus stop and began the eight-hour ride to Port Mariel. The countryside rolled by. All lush forests and tall swaying trees. They talked little, which was unusual, but simply stared outside at the unfamiliar landscape.

"Nilda, this is it. We're leaving everything." Mariposa's eyes were moist, and her hands shook slightly. Nilda simply nodded, trembling a bit.

The sun-scorched military holding camp was called *Marielitos*, named for the hopeful travelers heading for the US. Spartan and bleak. Anticipation and hope filled the camp as new inmates waited to be called. They allocated the girls one of the numerous olive-green tents within a designated fenced-off beach area.

"Nilda, we have to wash. I can smell myself and you too," she said with a grim smile. "Our clothes are filthy."

"The guards told me the showers were over toward the beach, but he had a funny look on his face when he said it," Nilda said. The girls walked toward the showers and found them right next door to the toilets.

Mariposa waved her hand frantically in front of her face and all around her head, trying to escape the swarming flies. She gagged and stumbled toward the showers. Nilda tugged her away. This was too much.

Nilda pointed and said, "Let's bathe in the ocean." They headed away from the showers and toward the ocean. This seemed a great alternative until a guard in a camouflaged uniform ran toward them on an intercept path.

"You two. Get away from there!" the guard shouted, waving his gun around, giving them a fearsome frown. As the young girls turned in retreat, his chest puffed out and his shoulders went back in pride at a job well done.

The girls went back to their tent and laid down, exhausted by the heat and a little traumatized by having a guard wave a gun at them. Three hot and muggy days followed. They spent their time walking around the camp and dreaming of what their new life would be like. The girls stayed hungry, with the rations from the camp being Russian spam and water, of which they ate little. Finally, the call came for them to go to the bus.

They exited the bus clasping hands firmly to stay together. The docks were a scene of mass confusion, shouts and pushing. Soldiers directed people exiting the buses. They seemed to give conflicting orders, which added to the chaos. The sun beat down, hot upon the heads of the prospective travelers. Shoulder to shoulder carrying their bags, and determined to find their boat, the girls moved forward. Mariposa heard Nilda whimper more than once as people stepped on her feet or a sharp elbow jabbed into her ribs.

There were boats of every size and condition. Mariposa saw the flotilla of shrimping boats, recreational yachts, and tugboats alongside homemade flimsy rafts of inner tubes and wood. There were far too many boats to count, but she knew it was in the hundreds. With hurried glances, she watched the people as they pushed and shoved toward the motley fleet.

Mariposa missed little and, even in the confusion, noticed a row of large blue buses sitting ominously next to the far dock. With bars on the windows, these rundown and dirty buses had soldiers holding machine guns guarding their doors. The bus doors and windows were closed despite the heat. Mariposa held Nilda's hand tighter as she looked at the grimy buses.

A soldier came for them, yelling in Spanish for them to hurry up and come with him. Mariposa and Nilda saw the boat they were being herded toward. The boat was called *The Dulce I* and at the sight of it, their hearts sank simultaneously.

These two mountain girls had never been aboard a boat, but even to them, *The Dulce* looked dreadful. There were heavy wooden planks on top of oil drums lashed together with twisted jute rope. They had filled the open spaces between boards with chunks of Styrofoam. Black inner tubes were tied to the outside and bottom of the craft.

Their passage cost $500 each. Her Aunt had struggled mightily to pull this sum together. Other wealthier people paid up to $3,000 each for more seaworthy fishing vessels and ocean-going sea tugs—those without Styrofoam or inner tubes.

The boat was powered by a big diesel motor that, in a previous life, had been beneath the hood of a big transport truck. This motor vibrated the entire structure and belched black smoke. Mariposa's stomach lurched and her back tightened at the sight of all this. A fifteen-hour open water trip with these fumes. She prayed the motor would make it and that she wouldn't disgrace herself by vomiting.

Nilda's voice quivered. "Let's go back to Santo Domingo. This thing's going to kill us both."

Mariposa set her jaw and narrowed her eyes. "We're going through with it. Be strong, my cousin."

The soldiers yelled some more, and the boat started to fill. Several families went toward the bow, settling in the front of the boat. Mariposa and Nilda headed toward the stern, into the back corner, wanting to be on their own and out of the way. More families and singles crowded into the boat.

Finally, the doors of the dirty blue buses opened, and the organizers brought the last passengers to the *Dulce*. These were hard-looking individuals, barefoot, shaven heads, dead eyes, and crude prison tattoos. Mariposa's eyes widened in alarm.

Others were clearly unwell mentally, and some called out repeatedly, "Where is my doctor?" and "Bring me back to my room!" Unbeknownst to Mariposa, Fidel Castro had emptied the jails and the mental institutions of Cuba, happily loading them onto the flotilla, shipping these undesirable Cubans to his enemy.

The sun was beating down on them; humid and hot, sweat running down their backs. As they watched the new passengers with concern, noxious smells hit Mariposa and Nilda hard. Body odor. Urine. With all the smells wafting over her, and the vessel rocking at dockside, Mariposa worried again about whether her stomach could manage this crossing.

The boat was clearly overloaded, but it was time to leave. The captain pushed the throttle and the engine coughed to life. It responded with a shudder and an enormous belch of black smoke. Nilda and Mariposa realized too late that the stern area was a bad idea as the black smoke washed over them, stinging their eyes and throat. They eased away from the dock, and Mariposa looked across the boat. A pair of staring dead eyes were fixed on her. Her heart sank and her blood ran cold as the dark eyes watched her, unblinking from a jail-tattooed face.

CHAPTER 9
MARIELITO CROSSING

Gulf of Mexico, September 17, 1980

Dolores had paused and was looking at the still form of Mateus. "My Aunt Nilda raised me and never told me any of this," he said. "Tell me about the crossing," he said, instinctively knowing in his gut that something bad was coming.

Dolores nodded, face a sorrowful mask, and continued. Mateus shut his eyes once again, squeezing them tight as if to shield him from the incoming truths.

The boat had become an inescapable hell with sickening rocking motions, each creak and groan of the overstrained vessel sending fresh shards of fear through Mariposa's heart. She clutched Nilda's hand like a lifeline as they huddled in their miserable corner of the deck. The air was thick with the acrid stench of diesel and human despair, mercifully overshadowing the pervasive smells of body odor and urine. Mariposa looked down at Nilda, snuggled up against her.

"We should have brought your dog along," she said, to lighten the mood.

Thinking of her scruffy dog brought a smile to Nilda. Over the next three hours, the smiles dissipated as the wind and waves increased. It was difficult to understand where they were heading with no reference points, but Mariposa reckoned their sideways motion equaled their forward headway.

The ration of stale Russian spam and tepid water did little to quell the gnawing hunger in Mariposa's belly. The two girls had a small amount of ham and bread left from Santo Domingo, but they wanted to conserve that. They were also concerned about bringing food out into the open in the crowded boat. The rations were given out once per day, and there were hard looks to make sure no one got more than their share.

They were on the second day of the "fifteen-hour voyage". The girls did not know it, but they were still more than sixty miles from Key West. Their progress was slow, and they were heading much too far to the west. To make matters worse, the weather was deteriorating. As the third day of their journey dawned, wind gusts reached fifty knots. Powerful six-foot waves with whitecaps crashed against the makeshift hull and deck, spraying them with cold showers. The girls were terrified, clutching the side of the boat, their long hair whipping about wildly in the wind.

Mariposa clutched the black rosary around her neck. She intoned, "Hail Mary, full of grace . . ." with a sincerity and urgency she had never felt before.

Surprisingly, the *Dulce* survived the storm. It was more seaworthy than its Styrofoam and inner tube appearance would have suggested. However, there was water in the boat's bottom. The heavy planks had loosened, and the inner tubes had gone flat. Several people crossed themselves and reached down to give the boat reassuring pats, encouraging her to stay afloat and get them to Florida.

Nightfall came and, as usual, the boat was very dark, particularly in the stern where Mariposa and Nilda slept. Mariposa jolted awake to the sensation of a rough, calloused hand clamped hard over her mouth, stifling her screams. Another hand pawed grotesquely at her breasts, pinching and groping. She thrashed wildly, trying to bite, to kick, anything to stop the violation.

A sound came from one of the families in the front of the boat and the hands were gone. The assault finished. Mariposa lay still in the dark, shivering and not knowing what to do. There was no one except Nilda to tell, and her friend lay fast asleep beside her.

The fourth night came and there was no sleep for Mariposa. She lay still, awake and waiting, heart pounding. In an instant, someone covered her mouth. They forcefully took hold of both of her wrists. A hand moved at her waist and tugged her pants down. She kicked out hard with both feet and tried to bite the hand on her mouth. Someone landed a ferocious punch to her stomach and a hard punch to the side of her face. This left her gasping for air, the side of her face on fire and her ear ringing.

Mariposa looked across at Nilda, who was awake. Nilda's eyes were wide with terror and desperation, their pleading gaze reflecting a primal fear. All she yearned for was to evade the impending danger.

Mariposa had never been with a man before. Her mind desperately tried to will itself to another place, anywhere else. They left her in the back of the boat, bleeding, dazed, with torn pants, and a broken spirit.

Day five dawned with a bright sun. Mariposa lay unmoving in the boat. Nilda brought her the small water ration, offering what scant comfort she could. From the glances of the other passengers and Mariposa's black eye, there seemed to be an understanding of what had happened. No one was ready to stand up to these criminals. No one was ready to help.

The morning dragged on in a haze until the motor began making a dreadful noise. The shaking got even more violent than usual. This culminated in a loud bang and an explosion as the engine block cracked. Acrid smoke billowed across the deck as passengers screamed and scrambled. Water rushed in, the ocean itself reaching out to claim them.

Mariposa stared blankly as men rushed to bail and plug leaks. They were adrift with no way to control the direction or course of the vessel. The only positive from all of this was that the assaults on Mariposa had stopped. Whether it was the constant bailing or overall weakness, mercifully they ended.

By day eight, water was gone. Mariposa lay still. She felt hungry with a thirst that seemed unquenchable. Lips cracked. Tongue swollen. Skin dried and red, her anguish more than matched her pitiable physical condition. Her very heart and soul felt mushy and battered.

Fins were visible in the water as sharks followed them continuously. Two were bold enough to come right up to the boat, black eyes visible as they turned in endless circling. Their dead eyes mirrored the soulless evil of the men who had stolen Mariposa's innocence and broken her spirit.

Only three men had the strength to bail, and the water in the boat's bottom was rising fast.

When the Coast Guard ship appeared on the horizon on the ninth day, Mariposa felt nothing, not even relief. Numbly, she allowed herself to be hauled aboard and shipped off with thousands of other hollow-eyed refugees.

In Miami, the authorities housed and processed the refugees at the Orange Bowl football stadium. The processing was uneventful, and they went quickly to Miami's tent city, and then to their relative's house. The crossing was over, but its effects remained.

Not long after arriving, Mariposa's new life in the United States began with vomiting and clear signs of morning sickness.

Dolores ended her story and looked at Mateus, who sat with a creased brow and hard-set mouth.

"Are you okay?" she asked.

"So, I'm the product of some Cuban prisoner or a mental defective rapist." As Mateus processed the new information, he muttered, "It's a wonder I have any intellect at all, with genes like that."

Dolores reached out as if to touch his hand but pulled back at the last moment. "You have to write your own story. Your start doesn't decide where you end up."

Mateus shook his head. "Easy for you to say, but this is no Marvel superhero tale with a cool origin story. Rape, no father, mother dies when I am three years old, grandmother hates me, indifferent aunt raises me, poor as dirt and bullied at school. That is quite the start to life." To himself, he added, *And a mild cocaine addiction to boot. God, I need a hit right now.*

Dolores chose not to disclose the final brutal truth, that his mother, after surviving so much, was murdered. No need to rip open any more wounds. It was enough for one day.

CHAPTER 10
OF APPS & AFRICAN RIDDLES

Altadena, California, November 3, 2009

After an uneventful trip home from Cuba and several heavenly hits of his lab-made cocaine, Mateus was back in his comfort zone. He excitedly called his friends over to share what he had found. Muni and Tay sat eagerly in anticipation as Mateus laid out the letters on his small kitchen table.

The aroma of strong C-4 coffee filled the room. They added cardamom, cocoa, coconut sugar, and a dash of cayenne to their Blue Mountain brew. Mateus's right leg bounced, the cocaine vial nestled firmly in the pants seam.

The friends huddled around the beautiful cigar box. A regal Cuban lady looked at them from the lid, but the *Habana La Exportadora* cigars were long gone. They carefully opened and read the letters from Juan Mateus de Silva to his wife Maria Teresa, with Muni and Tay's Spanish proving good enough to comprehend.

Mateus was ready to show them the poem. He had reread it several more times and it still bothered him. He couldn't shake the sense that something was off, the phrasing too stilted and cryptic compared to his grandfather's usual eloquent style. This poem had captured his full attention.

Our Marriage

Our marriage, like a beloved cathedral in the capital city
Our marriage, like a lady who is the remedy of my life
Look, look, to this cathedral for the prize
Look, look, for it is there waiting

This cathedral, the biggest and best around
This cathedral, not quite the oldest around, is our remedy
Look to the crypt, entombed and waiting to be found
The treasure, the future for our marriage, is;

> *buried beneath the watchful eyes of Jesus on the cross*
> *guarded by our mother Mary who stands in the light of day*

> *Your Juan*

Suddenly, Tay stiffened, his eyes narrowing. Mateus watched his handsome friend, the dark smooth skin, strong nose and intelligent eyes. Short dreadlocked hair, the upper half of the right side dyed a blond color. His mouth tightened and his face reflected a focused, concerned look, with one eye almost closed as he looked past Mateus.

"All right, Tay, what is it?"

"Don't move," he hissed. "Someone's watching us." Mateus froze, heart suddenly hammering against his ribs.

"Where?" asked Muni, her spiky hair sporting different colors from yesterday.

"Front window."

In a blur of motion, Tay sprang up, his chair flying backward. "Who's there?" he yelled at the front window, falling naturally into a defensive martial arts stance.

Mateus looked and could see the silhouette of a tall man. His mind raced, calculating potential weapons. He did not own a gun, but perhaps a kitchen knife or hot C-4 coffee would slow the intruder down.

Tay vanished outside, bellowing challenges into the empty parking lot. But the mysterious figure had melted away, leaving only worry and rapid heartbeats in his wake.

"He was looking in at us. I could not see his face, but he was there for a while 'til I reacted. He didn't seem afraid and even his running away was a bit casual, like we're not the first apartment he'd cased." Tay's breathless words coming fast and in a pitch that was higher than normal. "Dude, you better buy a gun, or at least a big samurai sword."

Mateus shook his head. "I am more likely to hurt myself than the burglar. Why would anyone want to spy on us?" It was an unanswerable question for the moment. Tay's martial arts skills were formidable, but he wouldn't always be here.

Muni's face was scarlet; she was shaking, fists clenched. "Tay, are you insane? That guy could have had a gun and all your martial arts magic and special-colored belts don't help against that. What were you thinking?" she shouted.

"I guess I wasn't thinking. My training kicked in and I just wanted to protect you guys. My intentions were . . . umm . . . good?" He held his hands out, palms up.

As the adrenaline ebbed, Muni's shoulders relaxed, and her expression softened. "Okay, I guess, but use your head in the future. The bigger question is what he was doing there, and was it a coincidence that he shows up just as we are hunting for treasure."

"We're hunting for treasure? I have my computers and coffeemaker, but nothing else of value," mused Mateus.

"I have read enough fantasy and D&D books to know a treasure map when I see one. This poem is a map, our map!" said Muni, pointing at the letter emphatically.

They reread "Our Marriage" with a treasure map lens in mind. Muni thought the poem was clearly symbolic, and Juan de Silva wanted to tell Maria Teresa something private, something away from

Cuban Army censors and prying eyes. Tay wanted to take the letter to the chemistry lab on campus and run some X-ray diffraction and CAT Scan analyzes.

"C'mon man. This isn't the *Shroud of Turin*. It had to be simple enough that Maria Teresa could understand it," Mateus said.

"Hmm. Okay. Point taken. Clearly though, there's like a bunch of religious references. Think about the cathedral, Jesus on the cross, Mother Mary. C'mon Matty, this is right up your alley. You're the Catholic here."

Tay's right, as usual, Mateus thought. If he combined the simplicity needed for Maria Teresa, with the obvious church references, he ended up with a Catholic cathedral. A Protestant church would not have Jesus on the cross. The plain crosses they bore held a stark simplicity, devoid of the figure of Jesus or any other adornment.

"So, we end up with a big ol' Catholic cathedral," Mateus said, "probably in Angola. Wait one minute! In fact, give me an hour. Have some more coffee while I write an app." Tay and Muni looked at each other while Mateus raced first to the bathroom and then to his computer.

They had seen this before; boy genius gets creative spark. The result was usually a flood of impressive work in a short period. They chose to ignore the dilated pupils and slight tremors in his legs, telltale signs of the coke coursing through his body.

In thirty-five minutes, Mateus called them over to the screen, remnants of a lukewarm C-4 coffee in his hand and melting ice chips at his side. In a half hour he had created a database, complete with a slick front end. The program provided details for every cathedral in Angola. The user could query cathedral size, location, age, and other parameters. Pictures of the inside and outside were available with the touch of a finger.

The App UI (User Interface) was clever, if slightly sacrilegious. A smiling priest and obscenely curvy nun were guides to the database, pointing and break dancing over to the desired piece of info. Even

Muni, the hacker whiz, found it impressive.

"The Force is with you, young padawan," said Muni as she grabbed the computer to check the code. Her coder eyes flew over the programming.

"More like Jedi than padawan, my lady," Mateus replied, rightly proud of his creation. After Muni's quality control inspection, it was time to solve this mystery with this new program.

"Alright, time for more coffee and then let's dive into this thing. Some C-4 Blue Mountain coffee brain energy!" Mateus, still full of energy from his bathroom hit, went to the kitchen to brew some more C-4, and the three of them went to work.

An hour and several cups of coffee later, they felt like they had made no progress. They sifted through countless churches and debated each clue until their eyes blurred and their C-4 mugs ran dry.

"Regroup time," Tay said. "We should go back to the poem and reread all the other letters."

"How come?" asked Muni.

Mateus answered. "Because we are at a dead end and still don't know where or what he is hiding. My grandfather went to an awful lot of trouble to create this poem, write the letter, and get it to my grandmother. We're struggling with this kind of weird poem riddle and need something fresh."

"Guys, it's my turn," Tay said. "Give me the letters and twenty-four hours. I want to create a geographical timeline using the letters and then map it against the battles of the Angola Civil War."

"I only took thirty-five minutes," said Mateus with a smile, eliciting a Tay grimace.

"Muni, I will need your help. I sense some hacking in our future," Tay said.

They all were silent, thinking for a moment about what they

were attempting and where this would lead. Mateus felt a sense of inevitability settling over him like a cloud.

"Mateus. Matty," Tay said quietly. "You know what this means."

Mateus replied instantly. "We're going to need to go to Angola."

Flights and crowds of people all around. Cuba was bad enough, but Angola? He was not sure he could do that.

CHAPTER 11
SLIDERS & THEORIES

Altadena, California, November 5, 2009

The three friends gathered in Tay's Altadena apartment, adorned by an eclectic mix of African art and French Impressionism. A steaming mug of coffee sat in front of each, with a bowl of ice chips in front of Mateus. They turned the hi-definition big-screen television into their computer monitor for the moment.

The screen pulsed with a kaleidoscope of colorful battles and troop movements meticulously mapped across the Angolan landscape. Time stamps and GPS coordinates flashed in time with the battles. Tay had woven together an interactive timeline that breathed new life into the dusty annals of the civil war. With each swipe of the scroll bar, armies surged and clashed, each battle presenting animated 3D figures that represented troops, armaments, and equipment.

They played, moving scroll bars back and forth, watching armies and troops winning or losing according to history. It was almost like a video game with a predetermined outcome, worthy of a history major thesis at Cal State Bakersfield, Mateus reasoned.

"It's not bad," Muni said with a grin, watching the mesmerizing dance of animated skirmishes. After helping with some overseas database hacking, she had let Tay get on with it and was seeing the final product for the first time.

Mateus gave a slight smile and said, "Yeah, it's okay, for one day anyway."

Tay was immediately defensive. "Look, this information was tough to get, even with Muni's help. I had to get into networks both in Angola and Cuba to get this level of accuracy!" Muni and Mateus burst out laughing at his defensiveness, and Tay soon joined them, belatedly realizing the nature of their teasing.

Mateus finally asked, "Buddy, you're the best. This is incredible work. Super impressive . . . but what does all it all mean?"

Tay sighed and gave several more disclaimers. "This might not be precisely correct. Fog of war. Winners write history. Well, with all that being said, I have a theory. Just hear me out. The letter came from Luanda."

Tay leaned forward, his face alight with excitement. "There was no battle anywhere near there at the time, but surely the officers would visit the capital in between engagements, to report and to have some R and R."

"Keep going, and don't call me Shirley," said Mateus.

"Okay, Shirl. Colonel de Silva wrote the letter during the time frame between the battle of Tundavala Gap and the battle of Cuanza Sul. We can be pretty sure he wrote the letter in Luanda, and we know he died at Cuanza Sul. Look at this."

Tay's fingers danced across the screen, tracing connections and making the battles dance. "All indications from the troop movements and armaments used would lead me to believe he was at Tundavala."

"Even with the crappy interface, I agree with all of this so far." Mateus smiled. "We certainly know what we know in terms of Luanda and Cuanza Sul. The letters stopped after Cuanza Sul and the oral history, from what I heard at the funeral, was that he died there. I'm still not sure where this leads us."

"It leads us to treasure!" said Muni. "Look at the multiple times he mentions, *'The treasure . . . is buried, the prize . . . is there waiting, and the treasure... our future.'"* Muni smiled big, her creamy skin and colorful hair setting off her lively dark eyes. Mateus looked reflectively at her, feeling a chill dance down his spine, a sense of destiny growing inside of him.

Tay continued. "He also talks about a cathedral in a capital city. Given that he was in Angola, this had to be Luanda. It's the only thing that makes sense."

"Juan de Silva was this guy, a seasoned veteran, who had been in the country for years," said Muni, her eyes lit with a dangerous sparkle. "Something big happened either at Tundavala Gap or Luanda. He goes to all the trouble of creating this elaborate poem riddle. De Silva felt strong enough about it that he didn't want to write anything in plain sight. Too dangerous. Too risky. He found something, something big!"

This was familiar ground, as they liked to challenge one another on their technical and creative accomplishments. A long silence ensued. Muni moved sliders back and forth slowly for a time, watching the changing parameters. All three looked on with intense concentration.

Mateus looked down and said with burning cheeks, "There is something there. We need to go to Angola, but I can't do it. I'm sorry. Too many long flights, even with Muni's magic pills. The thought of being in that crowded city with all those people is too much. Just, no way." He looked up and said with a quiver, "This is a mental-health deal."

Tay and Muni gently tried to change his mind. They spoke of treasure and excitement. They spoke of family and connection with his history. None of it moved Mateus.

Mateus thought of his path. *Complete PhD. Work as a professor and research lead. Do this for thirty-five years. Retire.* This path definitely did not include treasure hunting and long, scary flights over the Atlantic Ocean. No way. He left with a heavy heart to prepare for class.

Mateus, who normally found the exploration of the relationship between the structure of neuron-like circuits in synthetic systems a special area of interest, struggled to focus on the subject. He was preoccupied and somewhere else. Even Starkey's rare sarcastic barb at the end of class barely registered.

Mateus arrived home dispirited, feeling like he had let his friends and himself down. Then the world tilted on its axis. His front door stood ajar, a violation, a menacing intrusion. His voice rang out in challenge. "Hey . . . you. I'm coming in!"

Chaos greeted him, a tornado of destruction. Someone had ransacked the small apartment; books scattered, chairs overturned. Couch cushions ripped open and stuffing scattered. Computer screens smashed and the desktop computer gone. The intruders didn't spare the kitchen, as they had emptied the cupboards and shelves onto the floor. His heart dropped, and he felt violated. Instead of fear, an icy anger grew in his gut.

Mateus stumbled over to his altar, relieved to find his mother's picture intact amidst the carnage. On the floor lay the rest of the altar's contents, swept off the table with indifference. But there, on the floor, lay a ghost from his past—a drawing he had made as a child depicting the Notre Dame Cathedral with long-dried drops of blood dotting the page. Mateus was brought back to childhood in Sharpstown. Back to the drawing. Back to the blood.

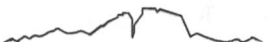

As a twelve-year-old, Mateus had a strategy for the school bus ride home. He tried to sit up front, away from the troublemakers in the back, and close to the exit. At his bus stop, he would rush to the exit and then run home. On most days, this worked. When it didn't, he usually took a beating. He was the wrong color—too light—and had the wrong accent—too Hispanic—and was way too smart in school. This combination made him an obvious target, hence the exit strategy.

The strategy failed on a sunny day in March. He could not afford a backpack and, instead, had a cheap blue two-strap canvas bag for his books and homework, the faded University of Houston logo almost unreadable. Four boys were waiting for him as he exited the bus.

"How was your day at school, *Seeñor* Brains?"

"Yeah, did you have a good day, *mi amigo*?" The bully shoved Mateus hard. Mateus stumbled backward. His legs were shaky, but he managed to keep them under him. Then the tormentors were on him, raining blows and kicks to his head and sides. Mateus knew from experience that a fetal position minimized his injuries in this situation. The bullies tired, and as they were leaving, dumped his bag out on the sidewalk. He slowly reloaded his bag while checking his body for injury. The blood from his nose dripped onto his papers.

Home. Clean up. Aspirin for pain. Make mac and cheese dinner. He worked on a science project while waiting for his cousin Nilda to come home. He put the bloody Notre Dame drawing under his bed as a reminder.

Mateus huddled on the edge of his rumpled bed, clutching the crumpled drawing as the memories washed over him, as well as the present situation. He thought about the contents of the letters and the poem. The treasure was perhaps out there, but more than that, it was almost like his grandfather Juan Mateus de Silva was waiting for him. As he sat, a new emotion stirred. *This is not a random robbery. Someone singled me out as the target. And, the treasure is real.*

It made no sense that anyone even remembered this treasure or that they knew he was searching for it on a continent so far away. Fear hit his stomach like an icy wave. But he was absolutely convinced that he had to go to Angola. For his grandfather. For the treasure. For himself.

CHAPTER 12
SPOILS OF WAR

Tundavala Gap, Angola, December 7, 1983

The Tundavala conflict was over, the dust from its battlefield still clinging to Colonel de Silva's uniform. With the ambush a resounding success, he strode confidently toward the Jeep with a satisfied smile. Major Perez and two elite Sombra scouts flanked him, and all quickly jumped in. It was time to find the UNITA commander, General Horátio Ilidio.

A sultry breeze surrounded them, the rolling dry hills covered with dry grasses and shrubs, which the Jeep navigated easily. No resistance; no one in sight. It was clear the UNITA forces had rushed headlong into the trap.

The command tent was easy to spot, the biggest tent, centrally located in the large camp. Weapons drawn, they advanced to the tent, a practiced formation with scouts flanking the two officers.

Inside the tent, chaos reigned. Two aides frantically worked the radio, their faces etched with panic and confusion. None of the radios were responding. It made no sense. A tall, gray-haired man in an opulent uniform was behind them, pacing and cursing in Portuguese. All three faced away from the tent's opening.

The colonel signaled to his men. In well-rehearsed steps, the scouts positioned themselves on either side of the aides. With a curt nod from the colonel, they simultaneously shot the two radiomen, leaving only the stunned commander alive. While the radio men crumpled, Major Perez quickly stepped forward to disarm the UNITA leader.

Colonel de Silva smiled coldly at the precision dance. He knew the game well; this enemy commander would have two caches of diamonds. The first, a petty reserve for local needs. The second would be larger with both the commander's personal stash and a supply used as currency for large arms movements in the area. He planned to find both.

"Sit," de Silva commanded in flawless Portuguese, his tone leaving no room for argument. Major Perez and the scouts melted away, and the two opposing leaders were alone. De Silva calmly and deliberately made two cups of coffee, sitting across from his adversary.

"Your army is destroyed," he said, each word weighted with finality. "Every single man. Dead. You are all that's left." A long pause to let that sink in, the words like a stabbing knife. "I want you to live, to see your family, to grow old. But first, we have matters to discuss."

General Ilidio went slightly pale, his hands trembling as he clutched his cup. A bit of the hot coffee spilled to the saucer and onto his hand.

"Please, colonel. We are gentlemen here. I have children, grandchildren even! We are men of honor, you and I. Surely, we can find a . . . um . . . a peaceful solution."

De Silva ignored this, his gaze unwavering, "Where are your *trocos*, your petty cash?" The commander immediately led him to a strongbox and deftly opened it. A handful of diamonds and stacks of bills were visible. De Silva gave a shout and Perez immediately appeared.

With a nod, De Silva passed him the strongbox contents, designated for the men. Perez smiled, took the bag of diamonds and bills, then headed out of the tent. He relished the act of distributing the spoils from their battles.

De Silva beckoned the commander back to their seats. He warmed up the coffee for both of them and sat down. Unhurried. "*Mi amigo,* we need to talk some more." His voice was low. Dangerous. Menacing. "I still want you to live. You have children to consider."

General Ilidio shook his head frantically, sweat beading on his brow and upper lip. "I can't. They'll kill me!"

De Silva shrugged, dark eyes stormy under bushy eyebrows. "Better later than right now." At the word "now" he rose and took a sudden step toward the hapless man. De Silva's right hand flashed forward in a blink. The commander's right ear lobe flew across the tent and his cheek opened up from ear to edge of his mouth, a bright crimson slash.

"Unfortunately for you, I am not a patient man. *Estoque grande, ahora* (the big stash, now)." His voice seemed to echo inside the tent.

It was a clean cut from the razor-sharp knife, but the cheek bled profusely. De Silva handed the commander a handkerchief from his pocket to staunch the stream.

Despite the attack, something about de Silva gave the commander hope that he still might survive this nightmare. His shoulders slumped and head bowed, blood dripping through his fingers and onto his uniform and medals. The commander pressed the handkerchief harder against the cheek and resigned himself to his fate.

The enemy commander stood and led Colonel de Silva to his personal tent. It did not surprise de Silva that the largest cache of diamonds would be in there. It was the rare and foolish soldier who would come unattended to the commander's tent. UNITA commanders frequently had guards stationed outside as well.

Under General Horátio Ilidio's cot was a dusty brown blanket covering the dirt floor. He drew back the blanket and exposed several wooden planks. He pulled out the wooden planks, revealing a trunk in a shallow hole. The chest was green and had two latches with locks. The commander stooped and unlocked the chest. He beckoned to de Silva to open the box, but the wily veteran shook his head no in case of a booby trap. Ilidio opened the box and stepped back.

A breathtaking sight. Ten bags, wrapped in oilcloth, each the size of an American football. The bags bore a stencil with the marking *UNITA* on their side. De Silva picked up one bag. It was heavy, about seven pounds. He emptied it onto the cot. Diamonds came pouring out, clicking and tumbling like a glistening waterfall onto the rough fabric.

The uncut and unrefined stones were a sight to behold, their raw beauty captivating. Sizable gems, sculpted into an array of geometric forms, lay before them. Among the collection, octahedron crystals were particularly striking, their structure resembling two pyramids joined at the base, with clarity and near-perfect symmetry a marvel.

Both men stood frozen, mesmerized by the sight. De Silva finally recovered himself and methodically went through the other nine bags. They were identical; seventy pounds of diamonds resting on the cot. He had also spied several pink diamonds big as a man's thumb. A king's ransom, indeed.

De Silva did not stop to think or let his emotions loose but simply loaded the diamond bags into a backpack. He looked thoughtfully at the commander. *Easier to simply kill the man and send him to the afterlife, along with all his men. No loose ends. Much safer and less risk.*

"Why so many diamonds?"

General Ilidio met his gaze and quickly realized he was bargaining for his life. He took a deep breath. "Listen, my friend. You said this was my chance for life. I have given up all the diamonds. These diamonds were meant to pay for a large UNITA arms shipment coming through Tundavala. You gave your word. Let me live."

De Silva said nothing but strode outside with the diamonds on his back. His men, who were well practiced at this job, secured the perimeter, swept for mines, and claimed any additional spoils of war. The discipline was impressive, as the men knew that arguing or fighting over spoils was a one-way ticket to a very unpleasant meeting with Colonel de Silva.

Major Perez took charge of the commander. The prisoner was

bound and gagged but not harmed, keeping de Silva's word to leave him alive.

As night fell, de Silva penned a heartfelt letter to his wife, Maria Teresa. His heart ached to share this triumph with her, a future now promising great wealth. But caution stayed his pen. Such secrets were too dangerous to commit to paper. He felt a deep love in his heart for her and, for the first time in a long while, longed to be home in his Santo Domingo.

Sleep claimed him quickly, the instincts of a soldier allowing him to snatch rest where he could. But even in slumber, his senses remained sharp. Sleeping lightly. Diamonds lying at his side. Dagger under his pillow. Pistol within easy reach.

In the dead of the night, the faintest rustle at the tent flap had de Silva's eyes snapping open, his hand curling around the hilt of his dagger. Danger lurked. Close by now. This quiet little night had just gotten a whole lot more entertaining.

CHAPTER 13
INTO THE LION'S DEN

Luanda, Angola, December 10, 2009

As the semester drew to a close, the reality of their impending trip to Angola sank in. Much to her disappointment, Muni was forced to stay behind, temporarily derailing her dreams of adventure because of a once-in-a-lifetime internship opportunity. But for Mateus and Tay, the journey was still on—a full month to unravel mysteries and poems and, perhaps, find a hidden treasure.

Despite his growing trepidation about the trip, Mateus had worked bureaucratic magic, navigating the labyrinth-like visa process with a deft blend of his Cuban heritage and fluent Portuguese.

Despite Tay's intense dislike for needles, the immunizations were all done—yellow fever, tetanus, hepatitis A and B, cholera, plus all the US standard suite like measles and mumps. They even had prescriptions for mefloquine or Lariam, a weekly pill that guarded against malaria, which they had to start early.

"How about that Lariam dude," Tay said, as they made their way to LAX. "I'm having technicolor dreams like I'm tripping on mushrooms."

"I get it. Me too. I . . . uh . . . well, I ended up having an unacceptable dream a couple nights ago. If it happens again, I'm done. Malaria seems like the lesser evil."

"Unacceptable dream?" Tay laughed. "What does that even mean? For me, the dreams are great, and I'm gonna kick back and enjoy the ride."

"Speaking of rides, I'm not looking forward to this plane ride." He patted his right front pocket and felt the pills there for the hundredth time. He also surreptitiously patted the seam on his right and left inside pant leg. This had been a major project for him, researching and then machining ceramic cylinders with screw-on o-ringed caps.

To remove any residue, the six thin watertight cylinders, filled with his cocaine, were boiled for thirty minutes after being screwed tight. The sterilized container was then dipped in a hot pot of a rubberlike substance that melted around the outside and solidified when cooled. The result, Mateus believed, was a dog-proof solution ready for airport security anywhere.

The flight to Dubai was a marathon, sixteen hours of recycled air and anticipation. Although Emirates Airlines was well known for their food and service, Mateus stayed away from the coffee and ate little. He buried himself in articles on cellular cytoskeletons, the dynamic network of interlinking protein filaments present in cytoplasm. Mateus thought that the way cytoskeletons moved cells could have application into reprogramming dead nerve pathways in stroke victims.

The time passed quickly. Tay made fast friends with the Emirates crew, his infectious grin on display, while Mateus studied.

Dubai International Airport was a world to itself, a glittering oasis of luxury and excess amid the desert sands. High-end gold. Jewelry. Brand name clothing stores. Mateus and Tay walked wide-eyed through the throngs of passengers, marveling at the colorful mix of cultures—African business executives in sharp suits, Indian and Eastern European families herding excited children, women in concealing black burkas, Middle Eastern men in blindingly white ankle length gowns with black *keffiyeh* headdress. It was a tapestry of humanity, woven together by the common thread of travel and adventure.

In the middle of the desert heat, the airport was a cool sixty-four degrees Fahrenheit. After a mushroom bacon burger and truffle fries, Mateus and Tay headed to the gate for the nine-hour flight to Luanda. They stretched their legs on the walk to the remote Gate D-21, where they immediately started sweating. The air conditioning was not working. The desert heat encompassed them and pressing in, an early "welcome to Angola" for the traveling students.

They flew on the connecting flight to Luanda in an aging relic of Emirates' fleet and much older than their first one. It was packed with Chinese workers, many of them clearly unaccustomed to air travel. As the wheels touched down on Angolan soil, plane still cruising down the runway, chaos erupted; men leaping from their seats, overhead bins spilling open, luggage raining down on startled passengers. Mateus and Tay could only duck and cover, exchanging bemused glances as the harried flight attendants tried to restore order. But they had made it to Angola.

Bodies and bureaucracy filled the immigration hall, a seething mass of chaos and congestion. Mateus and Tay were near the back of the queue, and everything moved slowly. The stifling heat and mosquitos permeated the un-air-conditioned space. Officials came forward and ushered families with small children to the front, which displayed Angolans' love of children.

It took almost four hours to get to the immigration official, an older man with white hair and a smock who looked tired, with bloodshot eyes and a scowl. Mateus' Portuguese, and he and Tay's Spanish, helped them get through the barrier.

They presented their yellow vaccination card and were let through, glad to have avoided the ad hoc yellow fever shot they had been warned about.

The baggage claim area was a hive of activity, with people scrambling to locate their belongings amidst the chaos. There were families with cardboard boxes for luggage, wrapped up with twine or duct tape. Individuals collected tires and other auto parts, either unavailable or too expensive to buy in Luanda. Chinese workers grabbed their baggage amid loud shouts while their supervisor herded them into groups.

Three haggard and uncertain expatriate families were moving to Luanda, each with over twenty-five large suitcases and containers, as they tried to recreate their US or European households in West Africa. Their drivers were grabbing bags to help, while their young children ran everywhere as the stressed parents scrambled.

Bags in hand, Mateus and Tay walked out of the airport, into the sunlight, into Luanda, into adventure. Taxicab drivers swarmed around them, shouting for their attention. All were eager to get the fare and be able to buy dinner for their family that night. Portuguese shouts. English. Even French entreaties. Air thick and hot. Crowds and drivers' shouting disorienting them.

The parking lot hummed with impatient cars moving in every direction and honking. One driver grabbed the handle of Tay's bag and tugged, trying to move it toward his car to claim the fare. Tay pulled back hard and held his ground.

Mateus tripped over his own luggage, almost falling to the ground. A striking young woman with a round face stepped toward them as he collected himself. Her bright eyes connected with Mateus as he recovered, seeming to sparkle in amusement and friendship. Then her expression hardened, and her voice rang out.

"*Sai daqui seu filhos da putas, agora!*"

Mateus caught the word *agora* (now) at the end, but the rest was way too fast for him. The drivers scattered, some quickly, others with reluctance, but all moving on to look for other fares.

The woman turned to Mateus and Tay, her smile dazzling against her smooth, dark skin. "I would be happy to give you a ride, my new friends," she said in perfect English, gesturing to a white Toyota sedan sitting at the curb. Mateus grabbed Tay's arm, and they headed toward the car.

They fought off a group of street urchins eager to help them get their suitcases into the car. The driver barked at the young kids, who gave her sullen looks but walked slowly away. Safe inside the backseat of the Toyota, air conditioning on and blowing cool air into their faces, Mateus let out a grateful breath.

The driver flashed a grin in the rearview mirror and said with a laugh, "*Bom dia.* My name is Romiana. Welcome to Angola!"

Amidst all the chaos, Mateus and Tay remained blissfully unaware of the watchful eyes of an ordinary man in a rumpled linen suit. After shadowing them from the baggage claim area, he slipped into his vehicle and sped up to keep pace with Romiana's car. His steely, unwavering eyes remained fixed on them through the front windshield, tracking their every move.

CHAPTER 14
NIGHT SOUNDS & LEAVING TUNDAVALA

Tundavala Gap, Angola, December 8, 1983

The faint rustling from the tent's entrance jolted Colonel Juan Mateus de Silva from his restless slumber. Even in the heart of a war zone, having a fortune of diamonds beside him was not conducive to sleep.

He cracked an eyelid and could just see a shadowy figure slip inside the tent. The glint of a long, curved knife in the intruder's right hand. De Silva's pulse barely quickened as the years of combat had trained him. A lethal calm. Soundlessly, he pulled an NR-40 knife from beneath his pillow.

His fingers closed around the hilt. This formidable weapon had been his for over a decade and was like a part of him. The Soviet blade, an extension of his arm, was six inches of razor-sharp steel ending in a clip point, perfectly balanced for slashing and stabbing.

De Silva prepared for the moment, rehearsed it in his mind, mentally practicing the choreography of what was about to happen. The intruder crept closer in silence as de Silva watched his silhouette against the outside campfire. Finally, the silent hitman stood above him, looming.

A flicker of hesitation, the man gauging his target's prone position to ensure a precise killing stroke. And then the knife flashed toward de Silva's throat. Arching downward. A silver streak of death, only to slide through empty canvas as de Silva sprang away in a blur of motion. De Silva landed in a crouched position, firmly on his two feet. Coiled muscles launched him upwards, the NR-40 moving at terrific speed.

The point struck in and up forcefully into the intruder's throat, producing a crimson fountain. Left slash. Right. Left again. Arteries and tendons parted as de Silva clamped onto the attacker's knife arm. A last gurgle. Then silence.

A fountain of warm blood covered him and his cot, dripping slowly onto the tent floor. This was the enemy, but de Silva still made the sign of the cross over the dead man. He sagged heavily onto the cot, carefully cleaned his knife, and then dragged the body out of the tent.

In the campfire's light, he could make out the man's features. Lieutenant Pinto, a recent arrival to the company. De Silva's face twisted in frustration and thought.

The word was clearly out around the camp and these diamonds were already extracting a terrible price, too much temptation even for his loyal troops. In a company this large, there were always some rotten apples. Perhaps he should have killed that pompous Horátio the moment he'd found the gleaming stones. Honor be damned. Impractical. Dangerous. Dumb, carrying these diamonds all over battlefield Angola.

What if he died? He'd sacrificed his family for his career. Wife Maria Teresa and his little Mariposa living in poverty, their faces fading a bit in his memory, if he was honest. Guilt washed over him.

Career over family. Promotions over visits home. Was this the correct way of things? Had he gotten his life wrong? He had to hide these diamonds, safeguard them. And he had to make sure Maria Teresa knew the location in case he was killed. This would change their lives. Maybe make up somehow for his long absence.

De Silva hatched a desperate scheme. He would hide the diamonds, notify Maria Teresa as to their whereabouts, and hopefully survive the war. In a war-ravaged hellscape like Angola, banks and safety deposit boxes were a laughable fiction. His mind kept going back to Catholic cathedrals, a place where he spent most Sundays.

De Silva wrote a detailed letter to Maria Teresa, describing what he had found and where he planned to hide the treasure. He expressed his love for her and how this treasure was a new beginning for them. De Silva posted the letter and got back to work. A sense of urgency prevailed, as they would leave soon from Tundavala.

His company was on the move, with orders to move to the Cuanza Sul Province and serve under the command of the enigmatic Generalissimo Américo. New in country and already with a reputation for poor command decisions, de Silva felt uneasy, a growing dread in the pit of his stomach. De Silva said a quick Hail Mary and prayed again for a promotion to general.

With his battalion on the move to link up with the forces of Generalissimo Américo, time was running out. He was to leave today, meeting Américo in Luanda before rejoining his army. Major Perez would take charge while he was away. The two had a lengthy conversation about formations, guard rotations, and other important details. These measures would ensure the army's safety and well-being in the upcoming battle.

News arrived that the mail truck, which was carrying de Silva's letter, had been ambushed and destroyed while driving to Luanda. *Could someone have read the letter?* De Silva hastily scrawled out new instructions to his wife, using oblique references and poetic allusions only she would decipher. He swore out loud, cursing his foolishness for writing the first letter so literally. Sealing the envelope with a hasty kiss, it was time to go.

The helicopter blades whirred, and de Silva ran toward the open door, dust swirling around his legs, his pressed fatigues flapping in the wind. Shielding his face with the crook of his elbow, he squinted at the Soviet Mi-24 Hind helicopter gunship that would take him to

Luanda. He clambered into the spartan bay behind the twin stubby wings. The side door gunner flashed de Silva a gap-toothed grin from behind a YakB machine gun which could deliver four thousand rounds a minute. He would be safe enough in this rig.

The Hind smoothly lifted off and de Silva stared out the window. His thoughts turned to the diamonds as he watched the magnificent Tundavala Gap scenery fade into the distance.

CHAPTER 15
FOLLOWED

Luanda, Angola, December 10, 2009

Their sedan inched forward at a glacial pace in the Luanda airport traffic. After thirty minutes, they made it to the exit. The secondary roads were no better, bumper to bumper, with progress measured in inches and feet. Luanda fascinated Mateus, despite his travel fog and exhaustion. His eyes scanned in every direction, and he thirstily drank in the sights. Cars everywhere. Honking. Lurching. Inching forward.

Blue Toyota HiAce vans with white roofs—the ubiquitous *candongueiros*—teemed with passengers. Arms, heads, and torsos stuck outside the windows to make room and sip precious gulps of fresh air. These taxis made abrupt and unsignaled lane changes without regard to other cars. Mateus and Tay were thankful they were not behind the wheel.

Amidst the choking exhaust fumes, the streets held a never-ending stream of people. Men and women walked among the slow-moving cars, hawking an enormous variety of items. Toilet paper. T-shirts. Pliers and screwdrivers. Candy bars. Angolan flags. The vendors walked slowly between the motionless cars, looking inside pleadingly at the passengers, rapping on car windows for attention. Mateus could see some car windows rolling down and money passed in exchange for the items.

The two Americans took in the ramshackle dwellings, an endless procession of cinderblock walls topped with corrugated tin roofs. Barbershops. Makeshift restaurants. Animals of every description, even pigs, abounded.

Women had their babies with them, wrapped in colorful fabric and nestled on their chest or back. With indoor plumbing a rarity, Mateus saw the ladies carrying plastic water-filled containers back to their dirt-floor homes. Other women balanced multiple pots and goods for sale on their heads, heaped with cassava or special gourds, walking with a proud grace that was beautiful and unique.

The air sang with a hundred dialects and the pungent aroma of food cooked on the side of the road. Small fires made in steel car wheel rims, coals burning brightly inside the impromptu grill, with various meats cooking on the grating above. Women sat with legs spread, surrounding cooked meat in cracked pots and crusty bread on a small towel, ready to make sandwiches to order for workers or passersby.

Babies and small children were everywhere, seemingly jointly mothered by all the women in a particular area. Mateus watched all of it in wonder and deep concentration. He jerked a little when their newfound friend Romiana spoke.

"What are your plans in Luanda? What brings you here?" Romiana's melodic English had a pleasing Portuguese lilt to it. This was a reasonable question as tourists were unusual in this capital city of over two million people. Vacationers were rare here in a city where most struggled, post the devastating civil war.

Mateus answered in passable Portuguese. "We are university students in the United States who want to learn about Angolan history. We'll focus on the cathedrals here and also want to learn about the people and culture. We're looking forward to being here for a few weeks." Romiana's eyes raised appreciatively at Mateus's Portuguese, and she gave him a thoughtful look.

Mateus found himself momentarily lost in her radiant features; flawless skin burnished to a rich patina by the sub-Saharan sun. Gold-tipped micro-braids framed her high cheekbones, amber beads glinting like droplets of captured fire. A delicate chain highlighted the curve of her neck, drawing his gaze to the graceful lines of her clavicle. Her sparkling eyes and smile lit up the space around her. *God, she is beautiful!*

Swallowing thickly and encouraged by her eyes, Mateus asked, "Would you be willing to, uhm . . ." The long pause was uncomfortable. ". . . maybe drive us around some tomorrow, look at some cathedrals and maybe the Slave Museum?"

Tay flashed his friend a sly grin, enjoying the rare sight of Mateus being so off balance. He'd never seen the shy savant so smitten, so utterly hypnotized by a pretty face.

Romiana said, "Your Portuguese is quite good. It's a pleasure to meet academics so committed to learning about our troubled past." Her eyes twinkled. "I would be happy to show you around." They agreed on a time for their rendezvous the next morning.

"I have to ask, does every driver speak such good English around here?" Tay asked.

"It's unusual," Romiana replied. "I had the privilege of attending Agostinho Neto elementary and secondary schools and took English classes for over ten years. The language came to me pretty well. I also like to watch TV and go to the cinema, English speaking with Portuguese subtitles. That helps, especially with the slang."

"Your English is great!" Mateus said.

"Thanks muchly." She smiled. "I was lucky to have so much schooling. Secondary school is expensive here and few people can afford such a luxury. After school was finished, I worked for an American oil company as a geologist for five years. That was like my final exam, as English was the language of business there and I used it daily."

The small talk continued as she glanced out the rearview mirror, not surprised to see the two cars following close behind. This was not a city for high-speed car chases. No squealing tires or breakneck speeds here, only the sobering reality that some very dangerous people had the Americans' every move under close surveillance. This was not a city where you could lose a tail. It was not a city where anyone could get away from what was following Tay and Mateus.

CHAPTER 16
THREE COKES PLEASE

Luanda, Angola, December 11, 2009

Romiana was right on time the next morning and waiting for them. The jet lag was real, and heads were fuzzy, but Mateus and Tay were eager to get started. They had been wide awake in the middle of the night and had spent the time poring over their meticulously charted itinerary, a greatest hits of Luanda's most historic Roman Catholic cathedrals. *Igreja e Convento de Nossa Senh, Igreja da Nossa Senhora do Cabo,* and others. They buckled in, Mateus in the passenger seat.

As they wound through the congested streets of the capital, Mateus found himself once again captivated by the riotous pageant of life beyond the car windows. Women in brightly colored garb hawked their wares between the idling vehicles, infants swaddled against their backs like living treasures. Animated soccer games were underway in the narrow dirt median strips, where laughing barefoot children played between two goals of small rocks, joyful voices rising above the traffic noise.

"It's early, but the people seem busy, and already going at it," Mateus said.

"It can be a hard life. Starting early gives them the best shot for making money for their business." Romiana replied. "I want to take you to the shopping center first, then to the cathedrals as they open up."

Romiana took them first to Belas Shopping Mall, close to their hotel in Luanda Sul. This modern shopping center had some of the highest prices in continental Africa. President Dos Santos named the mall after his daughter Isabel, who was the wealthiest woman in Africa. The country's high tariffs, lack of local manufacturing, and logistical challenges resulted in exceptionally steep prices.

Inside the mall's Shoprite grocery store, Mateus's eyes widened at loaves of bread costing twenty dollars. Prices for produce and canned goods were similarly high. Mateus and Tay walked past elegant jewelry stores, high-end clothing, shoe stores, electronics stores, and a cinema. They bought nothing but went outside to get back with Romiana and continue the tour.

Romiana was talking to another driver named Fernando. He was wearing dark green polyester pants and a pressed short-sleeved white shirt, leaning against his white Hyundai SUV and waiting for his client.

As they were speaking, an expat wife came out of the Shoprite, beautiful and slim, with long dark hair. She had spent around four hundred dollars on the week's groceries for her family. Six street urchins clustered around her, all barefoot, dressed in hand-me-downs and tattered, ill-fitting clothing. She passed out boxed lunches purchased for them. They smiled and politely said "*obrigado*" (thank you). Fernando helped the woman load the groceries, and they drove off, heading back to Monte Belo, the company compound.

"Look at that, man," Tay said appreciatively. "She's making a difference. Not for hundreds or thousands of people, but for a few. C'mon somebody! That's a big deal."

"This will probably be their only meal of the day," Romiana said. "These kids know this dark-haired lady. They're here every time she shops."

Tay looked pensive as he pondered these words. The poverty he was seeing was clearly hitting him hard. Most of these people lived hand-to-mouth each day. Mateus was also thoughtful and counted his blessings in a real and new way.

Their first cathedral was *Igreja do Carmo*. The Church of Our Lady of Carmel loomed before them, its faded pink plaster shimmering in the midday sun. A carved Madonna and Child gazed down at the milling crowds from an azure shell-like alcove above great oaken doors. Romiana pulled up to the front of the church and shut off the engine.

This 1689 house of worship was a leading candidate, and their hearts beat faster at the sight. The courtyard and the area outside the church were busy and crowded. People were selling food in the courtyard, others simply walking in and out of the church. Tay and Mateus anxiously glanced up at the Virgin Mary and walked softly into the church, with Romiana waiting outside.

Two stone-faced men in suits with white shirts came up fast to Romiana the minute the two Americans were inside.

"What are they doing here?" The smaller and more rumpled of the men frowned at Romiana, his small mustache twitching and his lips curling down.

She shrugged with a nonchalant ease. "They're history students who wanted to see some cathedrals."

"You know they're a lot more than that," the man growled. "Quit messing around. Is the treasure in this cathedral?"

"I have no idea. They've said nothing."

The man's eyes narrowed dangerously. "You've got a job to do here. Fail, and your father will be extremely unhappy. And we both know what that means for you. Now, do your job."

Romiana took a deep breath and her heart clenched. Fury followed by grief rose up in her, her face contorting into a tortured mask. She hated her father, and her mother's death two years earlier was still a fresh wound.

Pushing aside a sudden urge to slap this fool's ugly face, she composed herself and replied, "Don't worry. They're starting to trust me. I won't fail." She paused and looked him hard in the eyes. "Threaten me again, you will have more than my father to worry about."

Mateus looked at the inside of the *Igreja do Carmo* in wonder. Blue scrolling tile work surrounded the altar and rose to six feet around the perimeter of the cathedral. The ceiling was an ornate fresco of red and brown, swirling and curving elegantly around a central painting. Carved statues of Mary and several saints surrounded the altar. It took a few minutes for Mateus and Tay to stop staring and sit.

As they took it all in, there were things that clearly did not fit with the poem. Maybe this was not "almost the oldest around." There was no actual crypt or specific spot where Jesus and Mary were looking together. The statues of them all faced the back of the sanctuary. They listened to the mass for a time but sadly concluded that *Igreja do Carmo* was wonderful but did not hold the Tundavala treasure.

They emerged somewhat dejected while Romiana stood calmly by the car, her antagonists having vanished. The trio talked for a while about going to *Igreja da Nossa Senhora do Cabo* (Our Lady of the Immaculate Conception), but the church founded in 1575 seemed an unlikely site. It did not seem to fit the poem exactly. Romiana whisked them off to the next destination.

The Museu Nacional da Escravatura (Angolan National Museum of Slavery) awaited, its humble exhibits belying the staggering human tragedy memorialized within. This allowed them to keep up their cover as common tourists. It also held intense interest for Tay. His ancestors were Ndongo and from Angola. He wanted to see this piece of his heritage. A part of his history was in this city, a part of this Angolan slave trade.

The National Museum of Slavery was located in a chapel which once belonged to Álvaro de Carvalho Matoso, one of the notorious Portuguese slave traders of the eighteenth century. Tay looked at the pictures and small exhibits with intense interest. These could have been his ancestors. He looked with moist eyes at people in chains and people being whipped and treated like livestock. Tay saw mention of Ndongo several times and his ancient family name of Kasenda, people conquered and sold by the Portuguese and Imbangala warriors and slave traders. He was quiet as they finished. Mateus placed an awkward hand on his best friend's shoulder as they walked back to Romiana and the car.

Trapped once more in grid locked traffic, a hot and thirsty Mateus spied a gaunt youth peddling chilled soft drinks from a straining rucksack. The bag contained forty pounds of canned Cokes, surrounded by melting ice. Rolling down his window, Mateus brandished a fistful of kwanzas and called out, "*Três* Coca-Colas, *por favor.*"

The young man was bony and thin, all angles, dressed in a stained sleeveless T-shirt and ragged shorts. A small, tight Afro framed his unsmiling face. Along with most of the people Mateus had seen in the country, he wore simple flip-flops. The young man reached into the bag. Instead of a Coke, a knife flashed in the Angolan sun. The knife was through the open window in an instant and pressed at the throat of Mateus.

"Wallet. Money," said the young man in broken English, wild eyes darting between the car's occupants. "Now!" He pressed the knife forward and a thin line of blood appeared on Mateus's neck. Mateus remained motionless, his fingers unable to clutch his wallet, currency, or anything else. His mind, ordinarily a powerhouse of intelligence and calculation, was a total blank.

Tay reacted immediately, self-defense training engaging, muscles tensing for a desperate lunge. A dive from the back seat to try to grab the knife hand seemed ill advised, and he dreaded the risk of what he was contemplating.

Romiana's voice crackled suddenly with authority and menace. *"Pare! Filho da puta. Pare."* Her eyes flashed dangerously as she continued in rapid-fire Portuguese. *"Pare agora mesmo, seu merdinha. A Empresa vai te matar, lenta e dolorosamente."* She glared at the Coke seller and would-be robber.

To the American's amazement, the blade withdrew as if controlled by an outside force. There was a visible gulp and the would-be thief's olive-skinned features drained of color, a sheen of perspiration springing to his furrowed brow. Spinning on his heel, the youth sprinted away down the nearest alley, Cokes and ice and even the knife spilling out on the dusty pavement.

Romiana calmly said, "You can pick up your Coke now. If you want."

Mateus sat in shock. Another part of his brain finally started up and was processing the Portuguese words she had shouted. They made sense, although vulgar, except for the "A Empresa" bit. This meant "The Firm" or "The Company" in English. He wondered who or what they were. An insistent ringing from Tay's phone broke the shellshocked silence.

"Muni!" Tay answered with forced cheer. "What's poppin'?"

"How're you guys doing?"

"Girl, we're fine, routine day here," Tay said, shaking his head as if to clear it. Mateus remained frozen, daubing the thin trickle of blood at his throat with a crumpled napkin, unable to speak.

"Great stuff. Okay, my little globe trotters, I've been thinking and cogitating. Internship is pretty easy, so I have the time. I don't think you should focus on *Igreja do Carmo*. Seems like it's the oldest and not 'almost the oldest around' as per the poem."

"Thanks Muni. Point well taken. Strike that one off our list and keep looking. Internship is easy, you say, but is it going okay?"

"It's okay, but I'm not sure I'm cut out to be in the corporate world. Regular hours, dress codes, office politics, blechhh! And my Hello Kitty and Star Wars decorations draw some side-eye glances. These are not the things I worry about when I'm doing my white hat hacking or working for my boys in Angola."

Tay laughed as he hung up. "Hang in there, girl."

Mateus kept the napkin pressed against his neck, even though the bleeding seemed to have stopped. He had to ask, "Thanks, Romiana. But, well, how'd you do that?"

"Oh, my loud voice scared him. He's not used to someone shouting at him like that. Confidence goes a long way, perhaps especially in dangerous situations."

Tay's eyebrows raised doubtfully but Mateus, still shaken, managed to say, "Well, thank you."

"I think it's enough for today," Tay said. "Let's make an early start, *mañana*. We'll visit *Igreja de Nossa Senhora dos Remédios* next (The Church of Our Lady of Remedies). I have a good feeling about that one. It's Wednesday, so we can attend Mass. And Matty can say his confession." He smiled broadly at Mateus, hoping for a return smile, but nothing would be coming from him for a while.

Back at the hotel, they had a sumptuous meal of Angolan food, including *muamba de galinha* stew, which Mateus hardly tasted.

Mateus lay back on his bed that evening. The robbery lingered in his thoughts, and Romiana's words were like a broken record playing on an endless loop. The scene replayed in his mind, knife at his throat, the thief's threats, Cokes spilling on the asphalt, his own fear.

And Romiana herself. This was an amazing woman, incredibly hot, the stirring in his loins unmistakable, even this many hours later. Still, he didn't understand why her words scared the robber so much. The power in them was unmistakable, but the fear was greater than just the sum of her words.

Mateus thought about the people in Luanda. The poverty he was seeing was overwhelming. These people had nothing. He had witnessed this day-to-day struggle for food and survival, such a contrast to his gilded bubble of academics and fancy coffee. Yet, their spirit was joyful and their love for one another strong. The faint flicker of purpose began to ignite in his heart.

The two late model Toyotas had followed them all day, watching with indifference as the coke seller thrust his knife into the vehicle. One of the Toyotas passed by the hotel for one last time before melting away into the night. The second car parked, its hard-eyed driver preparing for a long night of patient waiting.

Mateus and Tay would stay under watchful eyes. There was no escape from A Empresa anywhere in Luanda.

CHAPTER 17
A WATCHED GRAVE

Luanda, Angola, December 12, 2009

The blistering Angolan sun was already punishing by the time Romiana's sedan turned onto the cracked pavement fronting *Igreja de Nossa Senhora dos Remédios*. Mateus shifted restlessly in his seat, the ancient church's history churning through his thoughts even as the vehicle crawled through the midday traffic snarl. It certainly fit the criteria of "almost the oldest."

Completed in 1679, the deceptively modest structure concealed macabre secrets within its whitewashed walls—the decapitated head of Antonio Mani-Maluza, the vanquished king of the Congo, enshrined to ward off his reincarnated vengeance. The small but beautiful white church had a central arch that ran between two towers and supported a large, ornate, almost Celtic cross.

"Guess we can skip the Cokes today, huh Matty?" Tay flashed a mischievous grin from the backseat, his eyes twinkling. Romiana smiled, her white teeth flashing from the driver's seat.

Mateus gave a weak smile in reply, one hand unconsciously touching the adhesive bandage covering the thin crimson line at his throat. "Perhaps one cold Diet Coke on the way home. Just for you, buddy."

Mateus and Tay piled out of the car and onto the cracked sidewalk in front of the church's wrought-iron gate. They merged with the bustling congregation, headed for the cathedral door, and sat down in a back pew. The Portuguese liturgy washed over Mateus, ancient syllables invoking a bone-deep calm even as his keen eyes inspected every inch of the incredible sanctuary.

Azuleijos tile made of cobalt and pearl climbed the walls, while the ceiling displayed geometric patterns in lusterous dark wood. Arched windows let in shafts of African sun, augmented by chandeliers lighting the room for the two hundred kneeling congregants. The faint smell of incense reached them.

The calming space seemed to melt away Mateus's remaining tension from yesterday's events. Even Tay was following the mass, although a beat behind, his Southern Baptist upbringing not including kneelers or Hail Mary's.

Their worship faltered as the transept commanded their attention. Flanking the altar stood a pair of vivid statues depicting the saints Peter and Paul, each immortalized in a riot of bright colors. Both were holding books, with Paul holding a long sword.

Mateus looked at the words inscribed beneath Peter. The Latin *TU ES PETRUS ET SUPER HANC PETRAM AEDIFICADO ECCLESIAM MEAM* translated automatically in his mind to *You are Peter and, on this rock, I build my church*. Similarly, he read Paul's inscription in Latin which said simply, *Paul, called an apostle by the will of God.*

And surmounting it all, the Virgin and Child stood next to an exquisitely carved wooden Christ who hung in the agony of crucifixion. "Buried beneath the watchful eyes of Jesus on the cross," Mateus mouthed silently, the cryptic line from his grandfather's poem springing unbidden to his lips. Could the Tundavala treasure truly rest mere feet from where he knelt?

The priest continued in Portuguese. "Brothers and sisters, to prepare ourselves to celebrate the sacred mysteries, let us call to mind our sins."

As mass concluded, Mateus and Tay lingered at the front of the cathedral. The two paid particular attention to the statues and the carving of Jesus on the cross. Nothing stood out or seemed to fit Juan de Silva's poem exactly. They took the stairs up to the balcony, framed by two large arched windows, and looked out across the sanctuary. There was nothing. Another dead end. Shoulders drooped.

As they stood, feeling deflated, a parishioner went through a door on the right side of the cathedral. The door opened and the believer kneeled, crossed himself, and then exited. Tay and Mateus nodded at one another simultaneously.

"Jinx," said Tay.

"You can't call jinx on a body movement. No way, man. And I don't think jinx works in a cathedral, anyway."

"Yes, it does. You owe me a Coke. Just don't buy it while we are in the car." Tay motioned for Mateus to follow. Excited, their hearts raced, and backs straightened.

They entered the room and found a scene torn straight from de Silva's enigmatic verse. Jesus on the cross faced them, the large lifelike carving dominating the room. His head was bowed. Brown hair and beard. White loin cloth. Hands and feet pierced with the smallest amount of red. Pain. A sin bearing face.

They followed Jesus's downward gaze and looked at the floor. A single grave occupied the center of the floor space, taking up most of the room. The marble slab covering the grave was off-white and centered in the room. It had the patina of age. Six small vertical green plants in clear glass vases surrounded the grave, nature's promise of rebirth to come. A lone white marble headstone identified the occupant as a long-dead priest, doubtless an important man in the early days of the Remedios church.

And there, a standing silent sentry, bathed in a shaft of golden light, the Holy Mother gazed out from her makeshift altar. Shafts of radiance streamed in through a small window to bathe her porcelain features, glittering off the miniature crown perched atop her veiled head. Her white dress and red shawl gave her a queenly air as her angelic face watched over the grave.

"Buried beneath the watchful eyes of Jesus on the cross, guarded by our mother Mary who stands in the light of day." The words hummed with scarcely contained excitement as they tumbled from Mateus's lips. His eyes went to Mary, to Jesus, to Tay, and back to Mary again. "Tay, this is it. We found it!"

"Damn right we did," his friend replied, voice hushed with awe. He reached out to clasp Mateus's shoulder, dark eyes gleaming. "Can you believe it? Standing in your grandfather's footsteps, a half-century later?"

Mateus's answering grin faltered, a shadow of melancholy flickering across his aquiline features. "All the years he lost with his family, the sacrifices made. And for what?" Ever practical and not one to sit long with emotions, Mateus said, "Start thinking about how we can get this slab off the grave."

Tay nodded. "Hmm, a tomb raider in Angola. Not exactly how I figured this Christmas break was going to go. Don't you have some biomechanics you should be studying right now?" Mateus smiled again, and they gave each other a quick bro hug. Mateus broke off the hug quickly though, uncomfortable with the contact even from his best friend.

Tay brought out his phone and took pictures of the room, documenting everything for their planning and for Muni so she could help.

As the friends started back to Romiana and the car, Mateus turned back to the deserted transept. The sightless eyes of Christ regarded him from the cross, perpetual orbs that held neither judgment nor reward.

"*Até logo,*" he called back softly, touching his fingers to his lips before sketching a quick sign of the cross. "Until we meet again." The words hung pregnant in the air, a solemn vow between the seeker and the infinite.

CHAPTER 18
GETTING LENCHO DRUNK

Luanda, Angola, January 12, 1984

The stifling heat of the Angolan summer swathed Colonel Juan de Silva even as he celebrated Christmas and New Year's at the MPLA command center in Luanda. The festivities came and went. He felt hollow, consumed by emptiness, a longing for the irreplaceable companionship of his band of brothers and the warmth of family awaiting him in Cuba.

The month in Luanda was filled with both meetings and holiday celebrations. Américo, the newly minted generalissimo, was in charge, a fresh import to the country. As well as being new to Angola, in de Silva's eyes he was an inexperienced, ill-tempered, and vain leader.

"We have a chance to end this godforsaken war once and for all," Américo had boasted, jabbing a meaty finger at the map splayed across his desk. "Savimbi will be at Cuanza Sul. We cut off the head, and the UNITA serpent dies writhing in the dust."

Jonas Savimbi, UNITA's leader, oozed charisma and self-confidence. His troops loved him and Savimbi seemed to be single-handedly sustaining this never-ending war.

Américo's battle plan placed de Silva's forces in an indefensible location of high cliffs and a river cutting off tactical options. Américo refused to listen to de Silva, and it deeply frustrated the veteran colonel. Combined with his increasing feelings of loss and regret because of the separation from his family, this suicidal plan threatened his sanity. With each passing day, de Silva felt death inspecting him closely, its icy breath on his neck, the weight of its gaze boring into his back.

To de Silva, he knew he had to oppose these orders, this plan. He frantically considered options. He even thought of directly contacting Fidel but knew this was a bad idea. Américo was currently very much in favor, and de Silva did not think Fidel would appreciate comments on the golden boy's ideas. He had to try one more time to persuade the general.

Américo was sitting behind a large oak desk as de Silva entered. The colonel snapped to attention even as he looked at the general's light skin and powerful build, a huge weightlifter's torso. The uniform barely accommodated his massive shoulders and chest. Bright medals and ribbons covered him, with his uniform having the look of someone on parade.

"*Generalissimo*, thank you for seeing me." The general eyed de Silva suspiciously. "I know we have spoken of the battle plan many times. However, I took the liberty of sketching out some alternative deployments." De Silva willed his voice to remain level. "If we reposition my company along this ridgeline here, we can—"

"You forget yourself, Colonel." Américo's tone was soft, almost gentle, but his eyes flashed with barely contained anger. "You continue to try to change my plan. I don't appreciate that. At all. Your maps and fancy drawings will not change my mind."

Américo's voice changed suddenly as he stood. His chest expanded and his face reddened alarmingly. He shouted at de Silva, "I am a general! And you are a *coronel*! I am in charge. I give the orders, and you follow them. If you cannot follow orders, I will have you shipped home. Today!" A long pause. An irate frown. A scorching glare. "Dismissed!"

De Silva saluted and performed a crisp military turn, striding out of the room with his maps and plans under his right arm. Américo's hubris would be the death of them all, consigning his bereaved Maria Teresa and little Mariposa to a life of grief and hardship.

Thoughts of his wife and daughter consumed his mind. He missed them terribly and realized that while the end could certainly come in any battle, this didn't look good. The odds were against him. He had to get the treasure hidden in a desperate bid to safeguard them against his death.

De Silva's steps quickened as he made his way through the boiling streets of Luanda, past makeshift hovels cobbled from corrugated tin. The Church of the Remedies loomed before him, its whitewashed walls shimmering in the midday heat. A regular attender at mass, de Silva had long taken solace within its cool adobe walls, where familiar Latin phrases were a comforting cadence and balm for his troubled soul. Today was different. One part of his brain took part in the mass while one eye looked for hiding places.

De Silva looked at the small room on one side of the transept. After mass, he walked around the grave and looked at Jesus on the cross and Mary on the stool by the window. *Ideal. A hiding place.* "God-given" he mumbled and crossed himself.

"Padre Lencho," he called out, catching the arm of the parish priest as he made his way out into the main sanctuary. "Might I trouble you for a bit of spiritual counsel this evening? Perhaps over a drink?"

Lencho Munguia had been with the Church of the Remedies for over five years. Unlike many priests in de Silva's experience, he seemed to enjoy his congregation and was approachable, personable, and good to talk with. De Silva also knew that Lencho enjoyed a drink occasionally.

"Of course, my friend," said Lencho. "There's no better way to discuss theology than in a bar with a beer in hand. Give me five minutes to lock up."

The two men walked in companionable silence to the local bar, happy to be in each other's company. After some light snacks, they huddled over sweating bottles of home-grown *cuca* beer, content in the cigarette smoke and loud atmosphere.

Even though he was planning to break into the church, de Silva could not bring himself to lie to the padre. He gave a carefully abridged account of his mounting dread—the upcoming battle at Cuanza Sul, his simmering clashes with General Américo, and the specter of death dogging his every step. He asked for the priest to remember him in his prayers. A true enough request.

They moved on to spirits, starting with a Brazilian *caipirinha*, refreshing and strong. While his eyes remained fixed on Lencho, most of de Silva's drinks ended up watering the potted plant at his side. By the time the moon rode high in the star-filled Luanda sky, de Silva was helping the almost unconscious Padre Lencho back to the parish rectory attached to the Church of the Remedies. He carefully placed the priest on a humble cot, took off his shoes, and covered him with a blanket against the night air.

Silent as a ghost, de Silva slipped back into the sanctuary, pulling a rusty pry bar from its hiding place under a pew where he had stashed it earlier. He looked nervously down to the grave and then up to Jesus on the wall, meeting the eyes that looked down at him from the crucifix. He shuddered and crossed himself. Once. Twice. Three times. A God-fearing man and one who just might believe in ghosts, he didn't feel great about this.

The scrape of metal on stone echoed loudly in the church as he worked the edge of the slab free. He winced at the sound but could not stop now. Sweat poured down his back as he heaved against the unyielding stone, finally levering it up and back to reveal the packed earth of the grave.

De Silva was nervous about seeing bones or smelling decay. If he was honest, there was a small part of him that feared a skeleton hand rising out of the grave. In the end, it was simply clean and flat packed earth. Relief poured over him, and his clenched stomach eased.

Finished now, he grunted and maneuvered the slab back in place, carefully cleaning the area to leave no trace of his sacrilege. Crossing himself, the colonel stumbled out into the balmy Luanda night. His body felt fatigued, but an enormous sense of relief and hope washed over him.

He thought again of wife Maria Teresa and her future. Tomorrow he would be on a helicopter to Cuanza Sul, heading into a suicidal battle where he would try to keep his men, and himself, alive. Regardless, some part of him would endure, hidden here beneath the watchful eyes of the Virgin.

CHAPTER 19
OF FÚNGI & FIRST DANCES

Luanda, Angola, December 12, 2009

The setting sun painted the Luanda skyline, a shifting palette of crimson and gold as Mateus paced the confines of his hotel room, pulse pounding in anticipation of Muni's call. The chirp of his phone made him jump as they connected, and he quickly brought her up to speed. She had additional information she could not wait to share. The poem said, "the place that cures." The name of this church was Church of the Remedies, or said another way, the *Church of the Cures*. This was an obvious connection they had not spotted.

"It's right there in the name, guys," Muni crowed triumphantly. "Church of the Remedies. The place that cures. It all fits!"

Tay punched the air, dark eyes alight with renewed zeal. "I'm telling you, Matty, that treasure is as good as ours. It's the right church. Jesus is on the cross, and Mary is watching over it. We'll pop that grave-top, scoop up the colonel's treasure, and sip mojitos on the beach before anybody's the wiser."

"Whoa there, Roy Rogers. We don't have the treasure yet. We need to break into this church, pry open the grave slab, and dig to get to the treasure. And listen carefully, mate. Do all this without getting thrown into a dark Angolan jail. Not so easy." There was a long pause as he let this sink in.

"Easy," Tay sniffed.

"This is exactly what needs to happen," Muni said. "How do we do this? No way we work with the Catholic church or the priest. We will not get permission to dig into a sacred grave inside a historical church." Another pause as they thought.

Muni continued more quietly, "And you two aren't exactly James Bond."

"Listen," said Tay. "We'll need Romiana to pull this off, Miss Moneypenny to our dashing Bonds." He started ticking off the checklist with his fingers. "We'll need a ride to the church, a stepladder to get over the fence, a crowbar, and a shovel, and a dark night."

"Let's go with a bolt cutter rather than a stepladder for both the front gate and the cathedral side door lock," Mateus said, then paused. "Taking a step back, though, something about Romiana doesn't sit right with me. She seems amazing, but the incident with the Coke knife guy was weird. Did you see how little thief looked at her, Tay? Dude, that was genuine fear. We can't tell her about the treasure. No way."

A plan slowly took shape. A midnight rendezvous at the cathedral under the pretense of a clandestine memorial Mass for Mateus's dearly departed grandfather. He needed to be inside the church to carry out the ceremony. It was super important to his faith and was part of the reason they were in Angola. It was flimsy but workable, and the best they could come up with. This spy stuff was tougher than it looked.

They called and asked Romiana if she would join them for dinner that evening. She agreed and suggested a restaurant on the *Ilha do Cabo*, the narrow peninsula that paralleled the coastline and wended its way along the bay, beautifully lined with palm trees. The area had high-end clubs and restaurants for the well-heeled.

Views across the beautiful bay at night showed an illuminated city of light, rivaling the skyline of any city, a glowing Oz in West Africa. Mateus felt an unaccustomed excitement over the dinner, the chance to see Romiana in this setting sending an unexpected shiver through him. He debated taking a hit of coke to enhance the evening but decided against it.

The boys cleaned up at the hotel, taking a quick nap and waited for Romiana to arrive at seven. At the last minute, Tay said, "Look, Matty, it ends up I can't go tonight. I need to call my folks, and there are some ideas on finding this treasure I want to explore." Only Mateus would have been able to see the ever-so-slight smile behind the words.

"What. What is it?" His heart leaped as he realized this would leave him having dinner alone with Romiana. He'd never been on a date, let alone with someone, well, like her. Pressure descended on him like a weight, his shoulders slouching with the realization. "Perhaps I should stay with you. Err, yes. I think that's for the best."

"You guys go. Should be fun. Relax, buddy, and tell me all about it when you get back."

Mateus went down to the hotel lobby to meet her, butterflies in his stomach. She was wearing a body-hugging tight black floral dress, accentuating her curves. Her hair was up in a sort of Afro puff, the large ball held in place by a shimmering beaded band that matched the dress. For the first time since they'd met, she had on make-up, subdued, with her lips a dark, slightly purple shade. Simple leather sandals completed her look.

Mateus had never seen a more beautiful person, and he stopped, dumbstruck. His mind raced, and he scrambled anxiously for an excuse to go back up to the room to spend the evening with Tay. He needed that cocaine, the confidence it mustered.

Mateus slowly wobbled forward. His words came in a nervous torrent. "Tay's not coming. You look great. Where are we going to dinner? I have to go to the bathroom."

"Okay. Thank you. Tamariz on the *Ilha*. Toilets over there." Romiana pointed, replying to all four items with a grin, enjoying his discomfort.

He ran into the bathroom and carefully fished the cocaine vial from the right pant leg seam. The shock of it going into his left nostril hit like a freight train. Unlike a movie scene, he did not throw his head back in response, but simply smiled at his reflection in the mirror. His confidence soared, and he felt he could face this beautiful woman solo. A quick wipe and check for white powder residual and back into the fray.

They sat at the table together in the Tamariz, awaiting food. The small beach was a few feet away, and the Luanda skyline glowed in the distance. They looked together in silence at the red and blue colors sparkling from the tall buildings, beacons of prosperity and happiness. It was magical.

The Brazilian *caipirinha* drinks were set in front of them, glasses moist with condensation, the light green color highlighted by sliced limes and a paper umbrella. Mateus had also ordered a coffee before the meal, which surprised Romiana.

"Are you really going to eat the *fúngi*?" Romiana asked, a twinkle in her eye. *Fúngi* was a cassava root paste, a tasteless starchy staple of her diet, and many others in Luanda. She had seen foreigners eat it before without good results. It was a bit like wallpaper paste, made edible by a variety of sauces. Like many of her fellow Angolans, she had a fascination with the dish and warned foreigners not to eat too much, fearing for their digestive tracts.

"I'm sure it's great if you say it is. Excuse me." He ducked into the bathroom and splashed water on his face. *C'mon Mateus, you can do this. C'mon man.* His hands shook as he took another hit of powder before rejoining her at the table.

"I guess I'll like *fúngi*. I'm practically Angolan by now. No *problema* here," said Mateus, giving her a weak grin, his face and collar still wet from the bathroom run. She laughed, and it felt good. Mateus's nerves were still there, and he was on edge, but he was actually enjoying himself.

The food came, a whirlwind of exotic aromas and bursting flavors. Along with the *fúngi*, there were small *langostinos* (lobsters), silky plantains, tender grilled octopus and toothsome shrimp, mussels that tasted of the sea, and robust chicken in a fragrant *verde* sauce. Mounds of seafood rice served paella style, along with boiled cod. This was a feast, and they both dug in heartily, sharing off one another's plates. Mateus thought it was the best food he had ever tasted, although the rational part of his mind realized that this might have something to do with the company and the setting.

"This driving around looking at churches makes me hungry."

"For sure. Tell me about yourself, Mateus."

"Okay, I'll give it a go." Mateus found himself opening up to a degree that was unprecedented. What was it about her that had this effect on him? "I never knew my dad. Never knew anything about him, not even his name. My mom's name was Mariposa. She was born in Cuba and came to the US and died when I was young, like only two or three years old. Even though I never really knew her, I miss her terribly. Does that even make sense? I really don't have any family." His voice caught a bit, and he used a cough to compose himself.

Mateus looked down, noticing for the first time a big *fúngi* stain in the center of his shirt. He sighed and continued. "Besides all the depressing stuff, you already know I'm a student in California. Study. Video game programming. Coffee. There is not much left to know. WYSIWYG . . . what you see is what you get, you know." He pointed at the stain on his shirt and grinned. She laughed with him.

"I usually don't open up to people. Maybe it was the *fúngi*. What about you?" God, he was falling for this woman. *Look at those eyes.* His mind raced, picturing a long life together with gray hair and fifteen grandchildren.

Romiana paused as a yacht cruised past the *Ilha*, its lights illuminating a landscape of sparkling water and small wavelets. She looked off in the distance past the yacht and seemed to calculate. "My father is very difficult. My mom and me were treated badly. He's not a good man and still hurts a lot of people."

Romiana continued. "After a lifetime of abuse from a philandering father, my mother passed away two years ago. She'd been like some kind of invisible suffering ghost in our house for years and now she is gone." A pause and a sniffle.

Mateus ached to gather her in his arms to smooth away these hardships, but moved the topic away, hoping to comfort her. "Umm . . . do you have a boyfriend?"

"Not sure why I am telling you this, but I am divorced. I was in an arranged marriage to a man who was a lot like my father. My infertility and his affairs doomed us, along with my naivete. The Angolan culture places an enormous value on children. My inability to conceive devalued me in my husband's and my friends' eyes. Their view was that something was wrong with me, a past sin or simply bad luck."

"And you were working as a geologist this whole time?"

Another long pause. "All this happened when I was working for Chevron as a geologist for Block Zero in Cabinda. My work suffered, and I took a leave of absence. I have not been back, and for the last two years have reluctantly been working for my father. I don't have a lot of choice in the matter, to be honest."

"I'm sorry," said Mateus. It was hard to see her hurting. His whole body was leaning toward her in sympathy and, if he was honest, in desire as well. He remembered his earlier doubts about her authenticity and felt ashamed. *No way.*

"Dance with me," she said suddenly, rising in a fluid motion and pulling him to his feet. His eyes opened wide in alarm, and he shook his head. "No . . . no . . . no." Even after a couple of *caipirinha* drinks and the coke, this was a terrifying proposition. She was not asking though, and pulled him onto the small dance floor, moving smoothly and rhythmically to the music even while pulling him gently with one hand.

Gradually, blessedly, he found the rhythm, following her lead. Locked in her embrace, swaying to the plaintive Portuguese lyrics, Mateus felt his rational armor melting away, piece by piece.

It was the night of his life, and he wanted it to never end. Watching her hips sway and body move was intoxicating, and he wanted to kiss her, but there was no way he could do it. After a couple of dances, they returned to their table, Mateus shyly holding her hand.

"Romiana, there is something I need to ask you." He had to stay on task, escape from his feelings, and get this treasure.

Her obsidian eyes searched his, faintly amused. A slight nod.

"Tay and I need your help. It's a spiritual thing that involves going to the church at night." *Great*, he thought. *I am falling for this woman and starting out our relationship with lies. Good job, Mateus.*

Romiana smiled enigmatically, fingers toying with the hair at the nape of his neck. "Oh, professor," she purred. "You have no idea what I'm capable of. For you. Anything."

At a table on the other side of the Tamariz restaurant, a hard man with dark eyes watched the budding romance in silence. Nursing a single *cuca* beer all evening, the proprietor and servers knew enough to leave him well alone. The man sat still, unmoving. Unblinking. Waiting.

CHAPTER 20
GRAVE ROBBERS

Luanda, Angola, December 13, 2009

In the dead of night, Romiana steered her battered sedan through Luanda's twisting alleyways, the city's deserted streets dimly illuminated by amber streetlights. Mateus, sitting restlessly beside her, felt his pulse quicken as the imposing silhouette of *Igreja de Nossa Senhora dos Remédios* came into view. Tay sat in the back, comfortably amused. Mateus was not sure whether Romiana bought their story about a late-night Catholic ritual, but she was here, regardless.

They'd spent the day as tourists, enjoying themselves patrolling the stalls at the *Benfica* market. The market overflowed with Angolan handicrafts, and they soaked up the local culture. They bought a couple of small, colorful oil paintings by a local artist named Kabongo, along with a *pensador* wood carving, the Angolan national symbol, and something like Rodin's *The Thinker*. Two feet high with shiny black wood, the detailed ribs and spine dramatically jutted out from the body.

But as the car slid to a halt in the shadows blanketing the cathedral's grand façade, all pretense faded. At one in the morning, the *Igreja de Nossa Senhora dos Remédios* looked more than a little scary, all intricate carvings and towering columns. Long spidery shadows, dying plants, and scattered trash in the courtyard added to the creepy atmosphere.

As they exited the car, Romiana stopped. "Listen, guys. Whatever you're mixed-up in is dangerous. I'm not sure how it will go or if I can protect you. There are forces at work, bigger than any of us." Her voice trailed off.

Tay leaned forward. "I can take care of myself and Matty. Don't worry." His chest puffed out, one hand made a fist, and his feet shifted into a martial arts stance.

Mateus squeezed her hand, and even with nerves and brain on high alert, he noticed the softness of her skin. "We'll be extra careful. Call us if you see anything unusual, and keep your eyes peeled. Anything seems off, you get out of here. Don't look back." Their eyes locked in a smoldering gaze.

"Let's move," whispered Tay, and the two Americans ran, slipping out into the muggy night air. They crouched low, darting toward the rusted gate guarding the cathedral annex. They shivered with nerves despite the warm night. Mateus's brain was working overtime digesting Romiana's cryptic warning. *Angolan prison for breaking and entering.* Colonel de Silva, his grandfather. *God, I need a hit.* His skin itched with desire, but this was not the time or place for cocaine.

Mateus held up the bolt cutters. "Listen, Tay. Last chance to back out," he whispered. "This is the point of no return for us, crossing the Rubicon. Breaking and entering. Get caught and we're in an Angolan jail for God knows how long." Mateus looked at Tay intently. "At least go back to the car and let me do this on my own."

His friend simply grinned, teeth flashing in the gloom. "Fortune favors the bold. We've talked about this, Matty. Your grandpa put this treasure here for you. No turning back. Now suck it up, buttercup." He put out his fist for Mateus to bump. Mateus managed a fist and a weak return bump.

The screech of parting metal sounded impossibly loud in the darkness, and they looked around for any unexpected visitors. Through the gate quickly, they were soon inside the church, shadows dancing as their flashlights played across the walls. Moving shadows. Catholic imagery. Gothic décor. A cloying smell of incense.

Mateus shuddered and just breathed for a moment, letting the centuries-old vibe wash over him. Heart still pumping hard, his courage building. Tay prodded Mateus forward, the professor's feet leaden with some kind of primeval dread.

They tiptoed quietly to the side room and stood next to the tomb. "A room with a grave. Late at night. Creepy church. Matty, it doesn't get better than this. And I paid to go into haunted houses at Halloween as a teenager." Tay managed a smile to relax his friend.

The light from the moon and stars beamed through the window, illuminating the Virgin Mary, who seemed to watch them as they prepared to desecrate a grave. Jesus on the cross was also looking down, and Mateus imagined a slight frown on his face directed at them. Mateus brought the old jet-black rosary briefly to his lips and made the sign of the cross. He was sweaty, and his hands shook. *Matty, best not to think, just act, just move.*

Tay worked the crowbar under the grave covering slab. He pried upward. Nothing happened. The off-white marble surface seemed permanent and unmovable. Mateus did a quick calculation, dimensions and material density numbers flying.

"The slab weighs about 547.2 pounds."

"Well, help me then!" came the urgent whispered reply.

Mateus stood beside Tay and added his weight to the lever. They were both sweating in the sultry night air, their muscles straining. *I've gotta start working out more*, thought Mateus.

The slab held tight for a few more moments and then suddenly shifted. Tay staggered back a step while Mateus fell straight down on his backside. Tay helped him up, their eyes connecting in the moment, a shared feeling of accomplishment.

They used the crowbar to force the slab to one side. It moved much more easily now that the seal was broken. Mateus mentally thanked Archimedes and his theory, thinking of his famous quote,

Give me a lever long enough and a fulcrum on which to place it, and I shall move the world. Lever and force calculations flew through his mind until Tay's words brought him back to reality.

"Matty, stay with me buddy. Shine your light into the opening." Mateus leaned over and trembled, not sure of what he was going to see. Bones? A decaying body? Snakes? He hated snakes. Or a giant pile of diamonds waiting just for him. *Flesh decayed at a rate of—*

"Today, buddy," came the urgent whisper.

Mateus illuminated the inside of the grave with his flashlight. Packed brown dirt, firm and flat, filled the grave, thankfully without bones or zombies. It had the look of a space sitting there for decades, undisturbed. On top of the brown dirt was a small mound.

Mateus kneeled and put his head inside the tomb, seeing a leather-bound book. The tome was weather-beaten brown with a rawhide cord wrapped around its circumference, which held the cover of the book tightly. Even in the limited light, Mateus could see the initials in the lower righthand corner of the book—*JAMS*. Juan Antonio Mateus de Silva, the initials of his grandfather. *Wow!* No diamonds, but this was still way cool.

Mateus reached in and carefully pulled the book out of the grave. He had just straightened up when they heard footfalls outside the room in the main cathedral. Tay and Mateus froze, scarcely daring to breathe as a dim outline became framed in the doorway.

The Americans looked on as the shadows revealed two men, one holding a knife and the other an aluminum bat. The intruders advanced a menacing step forward toward the paralyzed men. They wore black pants and jackets with white dress shirts.

Even in the moment and with his body frozen, Mateus's brain reeled at this departure from the standard Luanda street dress of T-shirts, shorts, and flip-flops. These clearly weren't businessmen, what with them holding threatening weapons. Weapons that might shortly end his life. His path to professorship suddenly seemed increasingly lame; his life on the line.

Mateus saw the knife and bat raised aggressively. The black-suited men leaned in, preparing to rush the Americans. Tay adopted a martial arts stance, hands up in fists, right foot behind left foot, slightly crouched. Mateus unconsciously put the book behind his back. He started to pick up the crowbar, reaching down, when a large black figure came flying into the scene, slamming into their two attackers, all three bodies going down in a blur of whirling limbs and chaos. Knife and bat skidded harmlessly across the concrete and away from the heap.

The newcomer pivoted and hurled the first assailant into the wall with a sickening thud. The other trespasser lunged forward, only to catch an elbow in the stomach and a fist to the middle of his face. He crumpled to the floor, and all was quiet in the cathedral again.

Their savior walked toward them, dressed in a black T-shirt and jeans, black Converse knock-off high tops on his feet. A large, handsome man with dark skin and darker eyes, he was not even breathing hard.

"More of them will be on the way," he said, eyes serious and shining even in the dim light. He pointed to the window next to the Virgin Mary. "Go out that way, now."

"Who are you?" asked Tay.

"A friend of Romiana's," their rescuer replied. "You need to go. Now. Don't look back."

Tay and Mateus exchanged a charged glance before launching themselves at the window. It would not open. Panic. Tay grabbed the pry bar. A stabbing thrust. Frantic lever. Window screaming in protest as they pried it open. Urgent shouts in Portuguese sounded behind them, spurring them on like the hounds of hell were in pursuit.

Tumbling out into the sweltering night, legs pumping like pistons, the friends made a sprinting beeline for Romiana's car. She scarcely waited for them to dive inside before stomping the accelerator, tires shrieking as they rocketed out onto the deserted avenue.

Mateus lay panting on the cracked vinyl seat, Colonel de Silva's journal pressed tight against his hammering heart. The car raced into the Angolan night.

CHAPTER 21
THE DIAMONDS START TO FLOW

MPLA POW Camp, Lugango, Angola, December 30, 1983

General Ilidio sat hunched on the rickety cot, manacled wrist chafing against rusted iron as he contemplated his once-pristine boots. The immaculate mirror shine was long gone in the middle of this makeshift MPLA POW camp. Now they were dirty, scuffed, and mottled with dried blood.

He sighed, thinking of his defeat at Tundavala. Not just the battle and all of his men, but especially the fortune in diamonds. He'd been so close to the kind of fortune that would make even his father sit up and take notice.

Tentatively, he raised his free hand to feel again the bandages swaddling the left side of his face. He winced at the pain and quickly pulled his hand away. *Damn Cuban bastard.* A tear rolled down as the loss hit him. His handsome face. All the ladies. Gone.

Ilidio's thoughts drifted unbidden to his father, Carlos Ilidio, whose shadow seemed to loom over his every waking moment. Now, he had to face both the women and his father with this wrecked face. His thoughts turned to his father and the military career that had led him to this cot.

Carlos Ilidio was a businessman, the head Angolan in a Portuguese import company. Carlos worked hard, enjoyed brilliant success, and made the family very wealthy. His son, Horátio, received fancy clothes, lavish dinners, every toy imaginable, and eventually cars of any type he desired—Maserati, Ferrari, Porsche—a striking contrast to the poverty surrounding them in Luanda.

The wealth was not what Horátio Ilidio remembered though, and for sure not the hand-to-mouth poor people surrounding them in the city. No, his memories were of the shouting, the beatings, and being told over and over again that he was not good enough. There was never an "I love you, son" from Carlos.

Horátio Ilidio was an only child with a mother that he thought he loved. His mother received similar violence, and Horátio frequently heard his father screaming at her. Outside of the beatings, his mother was very much in the background, invisible. She had little impact on him, like another piece of furniture in the house.

His mother looked the other way when Carlos came home drunk, with lipstick on his collar and perfume smells on his jacket. The servants ran the household, doing the cooking, cleaning, and getting Horátio ready for school.

Carlos knew Jonas Savimbi, the charismatic former foreign minister who headed UNITA. Savimbi uses his influence to get young Ilidio a position as a commissioned officer. Whisked away to Namibia, Ilidio completed a six-month basic training and three further months of specialized explosives training.

He thrived under the tutelage of the South African instructors, swiftly mastering Afrikaans, which delighted them, and impressing them with his cleverness. His father's discipline made him naturally neat and orderly, keeping his belongings and weapons in pristine condition. His dress, footlocker, and weapons were meticulously maintained, ready for the parade ground, inspection, or battle. He followed orders without hesitation, a habit from childhood to avoid slaps to the face. Horátio excelled at explosives, with instructors trusting him to practice advanced demolitions.

Upon graduation, Ilidio was a first lieutenant and placed into a logistics role. This was an odd place for an explosives expert, and he sensed his father's work behind the scenes. It was hard to get killed buying bullets and rations. Although Carlos seemed to despise his son, Horátio was his only heir. Depressed at first, he recovered and threw himself into the job. It all came naturally, and he very much enjoyed being "in between," between the sellers and the soldier consumers, in a space that allowed an ambitious man to profit.

This new position allowed for a lot of wealth creation. Crates could be lost, rerouted to waiting merchants in the city. Counts could be off, with payment received for more materials than were delivered. Ilidio kept materials moving, in a way that was better than any peer, but did not hesitate to line his own pockets along the way. He amassed a small fortune in diamonds while gaining a great understanding of how business really worked.

All seemed right until a fateful society gala at the seaside Hotel Carnival. Influential business executives and high-ranking military men mingled with beautiful women dressed in satin dresses and high heels. The buffet table held seafood and lobster, with premium steak and caviar, all served with champagne. Lieutenant Ilidio cut a dashing figure in his white dress uniform, pressed and spotlessly clean. He basked in the attention, eyed by men and women alike wherever he turned.

What an evening! He felt fantastic. Conversation came easy to him, and he circulated and mingled with many people, making connections. Unexpectedly, his father came later to the party. Carlos laughed with South African generals and Portuguese business executives, smoked cigars, and drank heavily. He seemed to ignore Ilidio completely. Horátio got up his courage after a time and moved closer, walking up to his father. He looked down, his shoes gleaming, pants pressed as sharp as a razor edge, and a chest filled with medals on display.

"Hello father," Ilidio said, looking his father straight in the eye, standing straight and wanting to look the part of a grown man.

Carlos looked back at him derisively and said one simple phrase, *"Fora de perigo."* (Safe man. Out of danger.) Carlos spat to the side and burst out laughing. He twisted away from Horátio, giving him his back. Horátio stood frozen and unable to move, stunned. He had thought his work in the military would be a bridge to his father. The dream was that they might talk together as equals. Instead, Horátio left the party immediately, deep in thought.

The following day, Lieutenant Ilidio put in for a transfer. There was a high-risk division of Army Rangers in UNITA who were always out front in battles or fighting behind enemy lines. With his record and explosives training, the transfer to the Rangers went through. He would show his father what kind of soldier he really was.

Many of the Rangers were South Africans. Ilidio quickly established a reputation among them as a good soldier and a fearless risk-taker. Most of the Rangers had nicknames, and Ilidio's was "The Badger" or sometimes "The Crazy Angolan."

In the Cunene province, he charged a machine-gun battery, throwing two grenades in succession and following them by jumping over a barrier with his AK-47 on fully automatic. It was a miracle he survived without injury.

He helped plan and carry out a mission to sabotage an MPLA artillery site. Horátio timed it so that the C-4 charges went off just before the start of the battle. This led to a huge UNITA victory and a promotion to captain. His squad was all Angolan, and they followed him obsessively, thinking him to be something of a legend.

Captain Ilidio continued to be aggressive, volunteering for the most dangerous assignments available. Over time and with greater wisdom, he changed tactics, and put his men in the thick of it, doing the planning and calling out directions from the rear. The aggression and results continued, but with much less risk to him as an individual. His squad had one of the highest fatality rates in the Rangers, but the stellar results overshadowed this. He made major shortly after that and was a man on the rise within UNITA.

UNITA head Jonas Savimbi had a diversity problem. He needed more Angolan generals in his army. There were still too many foreigners, too many South African leaders, and not enough nationals. Savimbi led UNITA and proclaimed them as the government for Black peasants. They were "for the people." Their constitution spoke of the representation of all ethnic groups. As such, it was important that his leadership had the right look.

Major Ilidio seemed like an ideal candidate for top leadership. The uniform looked good on him, and he was handsome. There were some good successes on his resume, and it helped that he was Angolan. They promoted him and put the newly minted General Ilidio in charge of his own battalion.

Ilidio wondered if this was enough for his father. There would no longer be any *fora de perigo* safe man. He was right in the middle of things. In fact, to his delight, he found himself in between once again.

As a general that meant Ilidio could arrange for the purchase and transfer of large, expensive equipment. This equipment was perhaps "destroyed" or did not make it to the battalion. The general could reroute huge shipments of food to an interested merchant in Luanda. Payrolls and expenses were hefty, and there were millions flowing around him.

The currency of UNITA was diamonds, and the diamonds were coming in waves toward General Ilidio. All the supplies and equipment were paid for with diamonds mined right in Angola. Millions of dollars' worth of diamonds flowed through his hands.

He thought to himself about the end of the war and his return to Luanda. Although no one was around, he spoke out loud, "When I get back to Luanda, I will use these diamonds to become the most powerful businessman in the city. My achievements will dwarf anything my father ever did."

And now this. General Ilidio sat nursing his wounds, beaten and diminished, his future and his father's approval fading with this failure. He looked again at his blood-spattered shoes and vowed to get the diamonds back, no matter what or how long it took. Trapped. Wounded. But he was far from broken.

CHAPTER 22
MAN DOWN

Luanda, Angola, December 13, 2009

Romiana sped away from the church, tires squealing and engine whining. They careened through the deserted streets of Luanda, her knuckles white against the steering wheel. The two Americans clung to their seats, hearts pounding in the aftershock. She finally slowed, breathing hard.

Mateus and Tay did not know it, but this was the first time since their arrival in Angola that they were not being followed or watched. No faceless observers or shadowy figures in the darkness. Alone. At last.

"What the hell was that? We could've gotten killed." Tay's voice shook with barely contained rage. "How'd you know that we'd need backup? Who's your friend? Who are you?"

Romiana remained inscrutable. Finally, she answered. "We need to find a safe place to talk. Explanations can wait." Her voice was even and calm, her small Afro blowing in all directions from the partially open front window. Even during all of this, Mateus could not help being smitten by the exotic beauty.

"The hotel's not safe. Not anymore," Romiana said. "My house is too dangerous as well. We should go to my friend Tomé's house. He's the one who saved your butts in the cathedral."

Mateus and Tay exchanged a loaded glance, unspoken questions hanging heavy between them. Trust seemed like a precious commodity at this moment of uncertainty. What choice did they have but to trust Romiana.

As they arrived at the front of Tomé's cinder block home, Mateus clutched his grandfather's journal against his chest, fingers tracing the weathered leather as if seeking some hidden wisdom. A silent, wry chuckle came from him as he thought about it. They had focused on diamonds, treasure, and fortune, but they had only found a simple book.

Tomé hunched over a rickety table, pouring steaming coffee into chipped mugs. His obsidian eyes glittered brightly and revealed little. Hard baked sugar cookies sat on a cracked, flowery plate in the center of the table. For once, Mateus drank the coffee without complaint or comment, a sign of how shaken he really was. They sat in silence for a few minutes, recovering, ruminating.

Romiana's voice cut through the heavy silence like a blade. "Talk to me, Mateus. And don't even think about spinning more tales of late-night Catholic rituals."

Mateus fixed his gaze on her, willing her to comprehend. "My grandfather Juan Mateus de Silva fought and died here in the civil war. We believe that he—"

Tay interrupted. "How'd you know to have Tomé on standby when we went inside the church? Also, how'd you order the Coke guy away? What is really going on here?"

There was a long silence. The night's darkness seemed to press around them. Romiana's shoulders sagged under an unseen weight. "There's a crime syndicate here in Luanda. Prostitution, drugs, gambling. They've got their fingers in all of it, even the people selling you Cokes on the street. A Empresa (The Company) is their name, and they are everywhere. They're watching you. Since the moment you arrived in Angola, they've been watching you."

"This can't be true, Romiana." Mateus shook his head. "We're just college students, nobodies. No one knows we're here. No way."

Tay's eyes narrowed with suspicion. "You must be one of them. Otherwise, there's no way you'd know they're following us."

"I know. My father, he's their leader. My father is the head of A Empresa." Mateus and Tay sat stunned. The words washed over them like cold water. Mateus's mind raced, calculating options.

Romiana continued. "Yes, he's my father . . . and I hate him. I want nothing to do with him, but I'm still under his control. A Empresa knows all about the diamonds, and you. They've known about you ever since your grandmother's funeral, Mateus. He's so crazy that he still had people in Cuba keeping an eye on your grandmother, after all these years. You showed up on his radar, and it's game on."

"And he's been watching me since then."

Mateus shook his head in disbelief. Tay scrubbed a hand over his face, the stubble of his beard rasping against his palm.

"But don't you see? There are no diamonds! The grave only had this diary, my grandfather's scribbles. It's just a family heirloom. There is no glittering treasure."

Romiana shook her head, her laughter a jagged, mirthless sound. "Perhaps, but it'll not be enough to convince my father or A Empresa. They are ruthless and won't stop. Once you're of no use to them they'll kill you both. And now that you've found this . . ." Her index finger pointed at the leather journal on the table.

The humid evening air clung to Ilidio's shirt as he approached, his normally impeccable suit disheveled from sprinting through the narrow alleyways. Across the street from the dusty facade of Tomé's house, four of his trusted A Empresa henchmen crouched with him in the shadows, one with a pair of binoculars dangling from his thick neck.

"Are they inside?" Ilidio whispered, trying to catch his breath in the stifling heat.

"*Sí, chefe,*" Suerte replied, lowering the binoculars. "Just like you predicted."

Ilidio allowed himself a tight smile. He knew it. There was no getting away from him. "What do you see?"

Suerte answered. "Sitting around a table, looking at some old leather book. Barely moving a muscle." The smile spread wider across Ilidio's weathered features as he processed this detail.

"Excellent. This is it then. We don't need them anymore." He turned to his men with a decisive nod. "Make your move."

Suerte met Ilidio's hard stare. "Standard procedure, *chefe?*"

"*Sí.* Kill them all." Ilidio looked thoughtful. "Listen, if you can leave the girl alive, then do it. But get the book no matter what. It's the only thing that matters now."

"You heard him," Suerte barked. "Carlos, around to the back of the house. You two with me, through the front. Let's finish this."

Tay stood, a newfound resolve etched into the lines of his face. "Mateus, we're done here. Grab the book and let's get the hell out of Dodge. Quick dash for the airport and hop the first flight out."

Mateus nodded his assent but unwrapped the leather strap and opened the book, flipping quickly through the pages. It was a treasure, even if it was worthless. Old battles. Family. Duty. Things that were important to Colonel Juan de Silva. Elegant cursive writing and highly detailed color drawings filled the pages.

Mateus saw a page with an amazing drawing of his mother, Mariposa, as a small child. A lifelike portrait of his grandmother Maria Teresa was on another page, a rare smile on her beautiful face. As Mateus thumbed through the fragile pages, a slip of folded paper fluttered and fell onto the table. Old and yellow. Frayed edges. It was a map.

Four sets of eyes watched in rapt fascination as Mateus carefully unfolded the brittle sheet. A map, sketched in faded ink and annotated with his grandfather's spidery script.

And there, circled in the margins like a promise, was Tundavala Gap. Eyes widened as this new revelation sank in. Tay opened his mouth to speak.

"Mateus, this means that—"

Gunshots rang out, shattering glass and splintered wood. Bullets flew past them like angry bees, pinging into the walls. Kitchen cabinets exploded outward, and chunks of drywall ceiling rained down on their heads.

"The back door!" Tomé shouted, jabbing a finger at the rear of the house.

They scrambled for the exit, crouching low and trying to keep their footing in the chaos. Mateus clutched the journal and its precious map tight to his chest, his field of vision narrowing.

A hulking figure loomed in the back doorway, blocking their escape, the silhouette of a revolver raising up towards them.

Mateus had never played sports or even set foot on a football field, but instinct took over. Without thinking, he lowered his shoulder and launched himself into the gunman. He slammed into the man with a block that would have done an NFL offensive lineman proud. The revolver flew up and discharged in a deafening roar, the bullet whizzing past Mateus's ear. The assailant crumpled, pistol spinning out across the yard.

They did not break stride, stepping over and on top of the downed gunman with churning legs. Romiana flung herself behind the wheel, frantically fumbling for the ignition keys. Mateus and Tomé piled into the back seat even as the engine roared to life.

It was only then, as they peeled out into the night, that Mateus realized Tay was nowhere to be seen. Romiana gunned the engine, but Mateus cried, "Wait! We can't leave him! We have to go back!"

Mateus felt the car's acceleration in his gut, and it threw him back in his seat. Bullets pinged the sides of the vehicle and then exploded the back windshield, showering them with jagged shards of glass.

Mateus grabbed the door handle, his face a mask of desperate panic. Even as he lunged for the exit, Tomé's iron grip clamped down on his arm like a vise, pulling him back inside.

Romiana slammed the accelerator to the floor, and they sped off into the night, tires squealing and the car shimmying down the street. Mateus stared in mute horror out the back of the car as the house receded into the distance, his best friend left behind.

CHAPTER 23
FACING HIS FATHER

Luanda, Angola, February 13, 1984

Horátio Ilidio's fingers trembled as he worked at the heel of his boot, the rough diamonds concealed within were his only remaining lifeline. With a furtive glance at the guards patrolling the MPLA prisoner camp, he pried the hidden compartment open and palmed the glittering stones.

A few whispered words with the more or less friendly guard at the MPLA POW camp and the deed was done. The diamonds were given to the grateful guard and in their place Ilidio held a handcuff key, a key to a nearby Jeep, and an MPLA jacket for disguise. Surprisingly, the escape was totally uneventful. This, along with the knowledge of what he was about to face, dampened his rush of freedom adrenaline.

UNITA had been quick to assign blame after the catastrophe at Tundavala Gap, the slaughter of his entire battalion, and the loss of the diamonds, squarely at General Ilidio's feet. Hundreds of lives lost. His reputation shot. Whispers of "gross negligence" and "dereliction of duty" dogged his every step.

After his escape and some cleanup, he reported to his UNITA superiors. He spun his story. "We lacked firepower, equipment, and training. We were up against a force with much better technology. We needed more air support and artillery placements, as per my request of nine months ago." His excuses went on and on.

It was all much too little and much too late. UNITA had been counting on the huge cache of diamonds Ilidio was holding, ready to pay for an incoming equipment transfer from the south. These were lost, all gone, along with his secret personal fortune, painstakingly amassed through months of skimming and smuggling.

Savimbi's rage had been terrifying, his eyes blazing in fury as he stripped General Ilidio of his rank and commission. They cast him out, dreams of glory and fortune evaporating in the hot Angolan sun.

The war was over for him. Fortune gone. He would need a new start, and he would have to swallow his pride and suffer abuse to secure one. Reluctantly, the defrocked general went to see his father high in his gleaming glass and steel tower. Horátio waited for forty minutes in the lobby before being called up. He steeled himself on the elevator ride up and walked toward Carlos Ilidio's office, footsteps echoing on the marble floor.

The senior Ilidio's office was a study in opulence, dominance, and testosterone. Mahogany wood paneling. Huge, imposing oak desk. Greek statue in the corner. Cigar humidor and drinks cart to the side. Pictures and certificates covered the walls, several of Carlos with various generals, politicians, and business leaders.

And there he sat, business suit and tie immaculate, head down. Carlos was seemingly absorbed in the papers on the desk. Horátio stood silent and nervous for several minutes, gathering strength for the emotional beating that would surely be forthcoming.

After a time, he said quietly, "Father, I am here."

"So, I see. What do you want?"

No *Tudo bem* (How are you doing?). Even after all he had done, all he had been through. His only child!

Horátio swallowed hard, fists clenched. "Father, I need your help. I need a good job to get started. I learned a lot in the army, and I can lead men. I just need to be given a chance."

Carlos sneered, mouth forming a cruel line. "You led men? Yes, indeed. You led a lot of men to their deaths in Tundavala Gap, didn't you. I gave you the perfect job in logistics. The perfect job to be safe and to get rich. What do you do? You try to become some sort of war hero and jump into bullets and battles. Dumb, dumb, dumb. You have your mother's brains, not mine." He shook his head, looked back down, and shuffled more papers, apparently having ended the discussion.

Horátio cheeks burned, fingernails biting into the palms of his hands. A part of him wanted to leap across the large oak desk and beat this old man to death, maybe with the big brass eagle sitting there to the side. He took a deep breath, calmed himself, gathering his thoughts.

"I fought for my country and for Angola. These are the facts. More than that, I can help you. Put me in a place where I can be your ally, your eyes, your ears. Do what is right for your only son." It was a long speech and well delivered. Carlos had not looked up or even acknowledged his son's plea.

For a moment, the air between them crackled with tension, the weight of unspoken grievances and long-festering resentments threatening to crush them both. And then, with a sigh, Carlos reached into his desk drawer and tossed a small brass key across the desk.

"The warehouse district. Building 17. You'll start on Monday as the warehouse manager. You'll report to me weekly. Verbally on Fridays and with a written report every Monday. Everything—and I mean everything—goes into the Friday report. Payoffs to A Empresa, kickbacks, my cut off the top, everything. The Monday written report will be official, auditable, and available to tax and government authorities. The warehouse will be expecting you on Monday. Your desk is ready, and your name is on the door." A rare half-smile at the end of this revelation.

Horátio took a half step back and stared at the key in his hand. His father was a step ahead of him, again, having anticipated his disgraced son would come groveling. Without saying thank you or anything else, the junior Ilidio left the paneled office. The Luanda heat hit him as he stepped outside, like a wall of moist warmth on his face.

Ilido closed his fist around the key, the metal warm against his palm. He thought about the warehouse, about being in between once again, and smiled. Somewhere, out here in this busy, crazy city, his destiny awaited. He would build a fortune, get the Tundavala diamonds back, and show his father once and for all.

And God help anyone who stood in his way.

CHAPTER 24
YOU ARE THE WIZARD

Luanda, Angola, December 13, 2009

Mateus sat slumped at the flimsy table, bloodshot eyes staring unseeing into the gathering dawn. He couldn't stop thinking about his best friend. Had Tay been shot? Had they kidnapped him? His brain worked feverishly to come up with something, anything, that would get Tay back. *I may have killed my best friend.*

Romiana sat beside him, lost in her own thoughts, her troubled gaze fixed on the horizon. She turned to study Mateus's haggard features and defeated posture. *What am I doing with this makeshift treasure hunter? This is the guy I'm going to count on? Burning bridges with my father, my ex, and maybe even my country? It doesn't make sense.*

Mateus was innocent, super smart, but clumsy socially, and on the dance floor. She almost smiled. He was kind though and definitely attracted to her and seemed like an honorable man. *Maybe he's worth taking a chance on. Maybe I'll learn to love him, maybe he'll love me back, maybe I'll get a share of the treasure, maybe I become independent of my father. That's a lot of maybes,* she thought. Still, a remote chance to get away from her father was enough. She was done drifting.

"Mateus, we need a plan," she said gently, placing a hand on

Mateus's arm.

Mateus lifted his head, a spark in his eye and determination that hadn't been there before. Excusing himself with a mumbled apology, he stood quickly and made his way outside. When he came back, Romiana could see his wiry body thrumming with energy. Mateus figured she did not need to know that his transformation was triggered by a half gram of cocaine up his nose.

"Romiana, think about how we figure out the location where they're holding him." Mateus's voice held a fresh note of command, the hesitation of the past replaced by grim resolve. "And get Tomé up from bed."

The house they sat in was under construction; blankets lay on top of a dirt floor inside a cinderblock room. A warm wind blew in through glassless windows, blowing over Tomé, who slept soundly, his soft snores rumbling over to them as they concocted a plan. Romiana woke him, and the three gathered at the table.

"Amigos, we're going to get Tay back. But we need to prepare, and quickly," said Mateus. "Romiana, I need you to use your A Empresa contacts to find out where they're holding Tay. I don't believe he's dead. Or I can't believe it. They'll want to keep him alive. He's their bargaining chip, something to trade with us. They'll want information about the treasure, and we want Tay. We have to act fast. What about talking to your father directly?"

"He'll know I betrayed him, but perhaps he will give something away or at least negotiate. I have to do this in person. I'm off." Romiana rushed off, deep in thought about how to approach her father and also the change in Mateus. The shy tourist and college nerd was gone as he forcefully directed the planning. It was attractive, but she needed to focus on Horátio.

As Romiana drove off into the brightening day, Tomé's voice cut through the silence. "Mateus, the three of us against all of A Empresa? That's suicide, man, plain and simple."

Mateus rounded on their ally, a dangerous calm settling over his features. "Then we even the odds. You must have friends, family, people who can fight."

Tomé shrugged, a newfound respect kindling in his obsidian gaze. "I'll make some calls. But this, this is the kind of favor that doesn't come cheap."

"I will pay them. I've spent the night with this diary and the map." Mateus's eyes flashed as he held up the items. "The treasure of Tundavala. I know where it is. You and your friends will be paid well if they help us. I give you my word. But first, we bring our boy home."

Mateus felt the weight of Colonel Juan de Silva's legacy as he thought of the diary's pages, already committed to memory. *Sun Tzu. Art of War. Duty.* One should always be prepared. Family and his little butterfly, Mariposa. A great man, a leader forged in the crucible of war and loss. Who was Mateus in comparison?

Tay needed a general, not a PhD candidate. He frantically put his mind to work, trying to produce a plan to save him. United States consulate, local Angolan police, Marines from the US consulate, hiring mercenaries, hiring Angolan soldiers. None of it made sense, and all of it would take way too long.

Mateus dialed Muni. "Mateus! How did my little hobbits do in the Church of the Remedies? Do you have Smaug's treasure?"

"Muni, they have captured Tay." He filled her in on the details of their situation. "I need your help to find where they're keeping him. What can you do?"

Muni reeled from the shock, the once lighthearted adventure giving way to a harsh and uncompromising reality. She pushed emotions aside for the moment and thought fast. "I could access the phone networks there and search. The two major networks are Unitel and Novotel."

"Okay. Do your magic and hunt for any mention of Tay or myself, perhaps even of treasure and Tundavala Gap. I would start there."

"I'll also try to trace Tay's phone. Maybe it's still with him." Her voice was husky with worry, her words coming with difficulty.

"Listen. I'm on this. I'm taking a sick day or a sick month from the internship to work on this. Whatever it takes. Leave it with me."

"Thanks, Harmony," he said, a rare use of her full name. "I got him into this, and we have to get him back out." He hung up.

Romiana came back three hours later. Mateus knew this wasn't good news. Her face was downcast, eyes hooded. "I tried all of my contacts, but they're not talking. It's clear they know this is big, and they're on strict orders." She sighed. "I had to go directly to my father. He was super upset with me and about the treasure. He would not tell me where they're keeping Tay. In between all the yelling, the good news is that they're keeping him alive for now, just like you thought."

Romiana paused, troubled eyes smoldering. "He wants to meet with you. Mateus, you can't trust him." Mateus nodded, deep in thought.

Tomé drove up with three friends in a battered old Ford car, its white paint rusting. They strode into the room through an opening where a future door would eventually be hung. The four were loose, joking with one another, with lots of fake pushes and slaps on the back.

Mateus went up to each of them and introduced himself, thanking each of them and shaking their hand. Tomé also brought food, which Mateus ate mechanically.

Mateus and Romiana talked as they ate. Romiana believed that if he attended the meeting, they would capture him too and possibly torture him. Mateus understood that but was thinking about a double cross. How could he set up the meeting and use it to free Tay? As he started to ask Romiana for her thoughts, his phone rang. It was Muni.

"Mateus! I think I've got something!" Muni said without preamble. "I hacked into Unitel and Novotel phone networks, placing some subroutines that searched for keywords. That's super slow going. It's a big city, and the pure volume of conversation is challenging. Then I had an idea. It was so simple. I should have thought of this from the start." Mateus sat at attention.

"I set up a trace and simply called Tay's phone," she said. "Someone answered it. I assume one of his captors. I used my . . . um . . . well, my female charms to keep him on the line. Think of Odysseus' sirens and their rocks of Scylla. Anyway. My charms kept him on there long enough for me to complete the trace." She could not hide her pride. "Mateus, I know where he is."

"You are an absolute wizard."

"Yeah, well, pay no attention to the woman behind the curtain, young padawan," she said, mixing genres and universes. "I have something else. Israeli drones protect the oilfields in Angola. These drones patrol the offshore platforms at night to make sure pirates or criminals don't threaten oil production. They control the Israeli drones remotely, which serve as the eye in the sky for all offshore Angola production. These drones are large, fixed wing, propane-powered aircraft with an eight-hour plus flight time."

At first, Mateus was confused, but then he understood. "Harmony Molly Kim. You hacked into an Israeli drone!" He could almost see Muni's beautiful smile light up from six thousand miles away. "You're amazing, and a siren to boot!"

Muni continued. "It gets better. You're right, I've hacked the drone. At first, I was able to simply intercept the feed. Watching oil platforms got old pretty fast though. Now I can control it. I flew it over the top of where they're keeping Tay. The drone was high enough that no one could see it. I got some pictures to share with you."

Tomé had a laptop with him and in moments, they had the pictures from Muni. They were staring at a large warehouse on several acres; it looked like a compound surrounded by a chain-link fence, with barbed wire wrapped around the top. The image clarity was incredible. They saw several small outbuildings on the perimeter, guards walking to and from one of the outbuildings. This was where she believed Tay was being held.

"Romiana, do you know this place?" asked Mateus.

"Yes," she replied. "This is one of the main compounds for A Empresa, on the east end of the city. This warehouse holds goods to be sold out on the streets. There will be heavily armed guards there, protecting the merchandise. I'm not sure about the outbuildings."

Mateus thought about the situation and tried to apply lessons from his grandfather's journal. Colonel De Silva was not here though, and Mateus was all that Tay had. This had to work. His mind raced through resources, the layout of the warehouse, and timings. He formulated a plan, a long-shot, high-risk, Hail Mary.

Keeping the doubts out of his voice, he said, "Romiana, tell your father three things. First, I've found the treasure. I know exactly where it is. Second, I want to give it back to him. It's all for him. However, third, and most important to me, is that Tay has to be unharmed and safe. Make sense?" Romiana nodded. "Now, let's talk about this warehouse."

Miles away in a grimy room reeking of sweat and fear, Tay's shoulder hurt like hell and was still bleeding through a crude bandage. He was strapped to a rusted folding chair, staring defiantly at his captor. Horátio Ilidio smiled thinly back as he leaned forward in his chair.

"Let's have a chat, shall we?" he smirked, the rasp of scar tissue pulling at his ruined cheek. "A little heart-to-heart, between men of the world."

Tay spat a glob of blood-tinged phlegm at his captor's feet, his eyes blazing with a brilliant fire. "Do your worst, ya sick bastard. I'm not telling you a damn thing."

Ilidio simply chuckled, the sound like crunching glass in the close confines. "Oh, my young friend, we have such sights to show you. Indeed, such exquisite agonies." The dark scar-raised skin running from ear to chin stretched as he smiled mirthlessly.

Tay set his jaw, steeling himself for what was to come. He closed his eyes and whispered a silent prayer. If this is the end, he thought, it's been one hell of a ride.

The first blow landed with shocking, brutal force. An explosive pain detonated on the side of his face as the world dissolved into a red haze of agony.

CHAPTER 25
INTO THE FIRE

Luanda, Angola, December 14, 2009

The blue, bright glow of the computer screen cast its light on Mateus's drawn features as he inspected the grainy images of the compound for the umpteenth time. The plan was bold, reckless even, a plan born of desperation and undiluted fear for Tay's life.

But what choice did they have? Simply walking to a meeting with Horátio Ilidio, the former general and son of a ruthless syndicate boss, would likely condemn Tay and himself to death.

Mateus glanced up at his ragtag band of allies, their faces grim and hard in the safe house's dim light. His heart gave a tug at the sight of Romiana, fierce and unflinching, forged hard from years of her father's cruelty. Tomé and his friends looked right back at him, hardened street toughs with murder in their eyes and pistols jutting from their waistbands.

"Alright, listen up. Let's go over the plan one last time," Mateus rasped, his voice raw. "Once we breach the perimeter, there's no going back. You four, make sure you stay well behind the cars. Don't expose yourselves. Romiana and I will be on the other side, by the outbuilding. We hit hard, hit fast, and pray to God we're not too late. Muni will run interference on the security feeds, buy us as much time as she can. But once the bullets start flying—"

He trailed off, unwilling to give voice to the unspoken truth that hung heavy in the air. This was a mission from which some, perhaps all, of them might not return. Romiana reached out and squeezed his hand, a reassuring touch amidst the gathering storm.

"Tomé?"

Tomé simply nodded, putting on a black ski mask. "Let's go get our boy."

It was late evening as they crouched outside the target. The compound loomed before them like a behemoth, all razor wire and soot-stained concrete showered in the sickly yellow glow of sodium lamps. Between them and the warehouse was a parking lot with no lines, housing vehicles pointing in all directions. An outbuilding, their target, sat alone to the right of the lot.

Presumably, Horátio Ilidio waited for them at the hotel he had designated. They had it timed to the minute. The rescue would occur precisely when he was supposed to see Ilidio.

Mateus's heart jack hammered as he watched Tomé's bolt cutters easily slice through the chain-link fence. And then they were through, fanning out across the weed-choked lot with weapons at the ready. Romiana melted into the shadows at his side, her presence a steadying balm to his jangled nerves.

Mateus drew in a shuddering breath, willing his hands to stillness as he thumbed the speed dial. "Muni. We're in position. Do it."

"Ready," Muni said, her voice a whisper. She accessed the security cameras. "Cameras going dark in three, two, one." Muni put the outside security cameras on a continuous loop, showing empty space even as Mateus's team moved toward the warehouse.

Two of Tomé's friends fanned out to the left, positioning themselves carefully behind large waste bins. Tomé and the final assailant ran stooped over to the right, hiding behind a blue sedan.

Romiana and Mateus crept toward the door of the small outbuilding where they hoped to find Tay. Mateus had Muni on speaker so that her timing could be precise for the next phase.

Mateus raised his arm, hand in a trembling fist. Tomé turned and pulled the AK-47 up to his waist. He yelled Portuguese curse words at the top of his lungs, *"Filho da puta! Cabrãos! Vai p'ó caralho!"*

His voice sounded incredibly loud in the still night but was soft compared to what came next. The staccato bark of AK-47 rounds was deafening as the assault team sent lethal bursts of 7.62 mm rounds into warehouse doors and windows. Glass shattered and lights exploded, with darkness falling over parts of the building.

When Muni heard this, she turned back on several of the outside cameras to show them a single crazy individual, waving a machine gun around and yelling curses to the sky.

Shouts of alarm and confusion rose from within the warehouse. The guards were well-trained, but no one could have expected such a brazen frontal assault on their own turf. The guards grabbed weapons and ran to intercept the assailant. Someone had to be awfully dumb to attack A Empresa. Suicide.

Mateus froze as one guard burst from the outbuilding, pistol glinting dully in the half-light. Time seemed to slow to a crawl, his world narrowing to the white-knuckled grip on his aluminum bat and the hammering of his own pulse in his ears. *Come on, Mateus. Come on. For Tay.* His hands were shaking.

In a single, crystalline moment of clarity, the countless hours spent poring over neurology texts flashed through his mind. The vagus nerve, that great wandering conduit that held sway over so much of the body's autonomic functions. A single, precisely targeted blow would yield muscle spasms and potential unconsciousness.

But then a guard was on him, pistol swinging toward his chest, and there was no more time for theory or finesse. Mateus closed his eyes and swung the bat in a wild, looping arc, aiming for the guard's head.

The bat struck the guard on the right shoulder. He staggered from the blow and dropped the weapon. Mateus's eyes widened as the guard staggered but did not fall. He swung a second time. Harder. Rage. He's my best friend. Eyes wide open. Impact to the guard's skull.

The sickening crunch of shattering bone echoed as the guard crumpled to the oil-stained asphalt and lay in a spreading pool of crimson.

The warehouse doors opened, and out poured ten A Empresa troops with pistols and AK-47s. Tomé scrambled back. He ran between the bins and the cars, toward his hiding friends.

The guards looked around for something, anything, to shoot. Gunfire erupted from all sides as Tomé's friends fired the shots. The guards raised their guns to fire back when a high-keening whine came from high above their heads, a mechanical whirring noise. The combatants craned their necks skyward, weapons falling slack in their hands as they glimpsed the source of the strange noise.

Muni sat surrounded by piles of Hebrew dictionaries, *Dungeons and Dragons* monster compendiums, and *Lord of the Rings* first editions. She hunched over a sticker-covered laptop; her delicate features bathed in the computer's light.

Her fingers flew on the keyboard, deft, blurred movements of precision and grace as lines of code pulled away the gossamer threads of the Israeli drone's safeguards. Muni's heart raced as the UAV's control interface came to life. Telemetry and sensor feeds laid bare before her.

She was soaring, an intoxicating flight above the streets of Luanda, the ground rushing past below, the speed of the craft and smoothness of the control surfaces exhilarating.

The drone hung suspended above the compound like a great predatory bird, its matte-black fuselage melding with the pale moonlight. Sleek and angular, all swooping lines and razor edges, it was like something alive, from a fever dream, a harbinger of death, a reaper on swift and silent wings.

And then it was descending, slowly at first, then with gathering speed, the whine of its turbines rising to an otherworldly scream. The once graceful flight turned menacing, and astonishment morphed into terror, paralyzing the guards.

The signal came from Mateus, and the fixed wing craft banked hard over the A Empresa compound. All her rage, frustration, and fear poured into the laptop's joystick, causing a primal scream to build in her throat. The UAV's nose angled downward, and the throttle redlined, propane-fueled engine screaming.

Tomé and his friends knew what was coming, scrambling back toward the fence and dropping to the ground behind protective cover. Mateus and Romiana did the same, crouching behind the outbuilding. The A Empresa gunmen turned to run, but it was much too late.

Willing their feet to move, the men frantically dove for cover, scrambling to get away. Meanwhile, the drone, accelerating to a staggering one hundred twenty-five miles per hour, bore down on them, its path locked on their position.

The world dissolved in fire and fury, a maelstrom of shrapnel and flame. Transforming into a menacing blue fireball of destruction, the explosion was awe-inspiring. Nearby cars ignited and caused secondary explosions. The force of the explosion tossed gunmen around like rag dolls and scattered their bodies over the lot.

CHAPTER 26
TAY'S TRIAL

Luanda, Angola, December 13, 2009

The day before the drone attack, Tay found himself at Tomé's table, the rush of their close call fading, giving way to a bone-deep weariness. As the map fell out of the book, his fatigue vanished as he immediately realized that they were back in the game.

He had smiled his "Tay smile" as Muni called it, nodding, his dreadlocks bobbing, when the bullets crashed through the front windows. The glass stung his back and arms, and Tomé yelled, "Back door!"

Tay scrambled to his feet, took two steps toward the back, when he felt a hard punch to the back of his right shoulder. The impact spun him around, and he crashed to the floor. There was no pain in these first moments. He touched his shirt and could feel the blood.

His friends were running out the back door. *Are they deserting me?* He could not believe it. He lay on the hard floor, feeling blood leak from his shoulder and onto the concrete floor. Strangely, there was still no pain.

Rough hands hauled him upright. Disoriented, he blinked away the fog and stared at four hard-eyed young men in cheap suits, utterly unconcerned about his wound. The A Empresa men walked him out to their SUV, sitting him in the backseat, in between the two of them. His mouth opened, and he tried to speak, but received a hard elbow to the side of his head in response.

No hoods. No blindfolds. The implication was clear. Wherever they were taking him, he wasn't meant to return.

The SUV's interior was stifling, a cocoon of leather and recirculated air, Tay's captors pressing in on either side like the walls of a tomb. His mind raced as he fought down the rising gorge of panic clawing at his throat. His cell phone was in his pocket, so perhaps that was something. If he could just get a message to Muni.

That faint hope died as they arrived at a menacing warehouse and marched him across weed-choked asphalt to a small building. The room was stark. Bare concrete walls. Flickering lightbulb. Rickety table flanked by rusted metal chairs.

They forced him down into one of the unforgiving seats, hands reaching for hemp ropes. They wrenched his wounded arm behind his back, and he let out a blood-curdling scream. He played up the injury, hoping they would leave his arm free.

The guard's eyes remained cold, dead, chips of obsidian within blank faces. Tay was sweating and pale. This part was not acting. They callously took a rag and gagged him, pulling it tight. They forced the arm back again, hard, Tay's very real screams muffled by the gag. These were men used to observing and inflicting pain. They were unmoved.

Tay's world had narrowed to the pain in his shoulder and the two hard men sitting in the room with him. After an initial conflict with the old man, the hard punch to his face shattered him and almost broke him. He drifted in and out of consciousness, surfacing only to be shocked to wakefulness by a deluge of icy water.

Sputtering and gasping, his gag taken off, he found himself face-to-face with an older man, graying hair atop a wrinkled face, a thin mustache. The once-handsome features had been ravaged, a cruel slash of scar tissue marring his visage from ear to chin, the surrounding skin puckered and shiny in the half-light.

"Mr. Altheas Jackson," the menacing man purred, voice smooth as oiled silk. "Or may I call you Tay. Let's try again. It's a pleasure to meet you. I'm sorry we meet in these circumstances. I'm also sorry to let you know that you're going to have to work very hard to come out of this building alive."

Tay swallowed hard, fear and rage knotting in his breast. "I'm afraid you have me at a disadvantage, friend. I didn't catch your name," he said cooly.

The old man smiled without humor and continued. "My name is Horátio Ilidio, at your service. I was a commander in the Angolan Civil War but now am the leader of A Empresa, a company that sells commodities to the citizens and comrades of Angola. You and your friends have something that belongs to me."

Horátio leaned in close, the stench of expensive tobacco and cloying cologne washing over Tay in a noxious wave. "The diamonds are mine. You are going to tell me what I need to know so that I can get them back." He paused, letting his words sink in. He seemed relaxed, with all the time in the world.

"Señor Ilidio," Tay began. "It's a pleasure to meet you." Tay's instinct was to be especially respectful. He knew from reading books and watching movies that while being tortured, it's best to tell as much truth as you can, because eventually they will get it out of you.

"My friends and I have been seeking the diamonds. We thought they were in the Church of the Remedies. It turns out we were wrong. We dug up a grave there and found a simple diary, no diamonds. Sincerely and respectfully, I don't know where the diamonds are located. This is all I know, sir."

Ilidio remained calm, grinning perhaps at what was next to come. "That's not enough for me, my friend, not nearly enough. Please beat him, boys." The guards worked Tay over with a methodical brutality, cracked ribs and flayed skin blurring into a crimson fog.

Ilidio walked over to the battered cabinet. From the top drawer, he took out several blood-stained knives, a pair of pliers, and a clamp.

Next, he grabbed a small generator that looked like a car battery charger, complete with two rusty electrodes. "I don't want to hurt you, I really don't. I get my diamonds and you all can get back on your plane."

Tay's chest jolted and his back arched. He bit into the piece of wood and convulsed. The electrodes were attached to his nipples with the generator settings at about half power. "I will ask you again," said Ilidio. "Where are my diamonds?"

"I don't know!" Tay was sweating profusely, trying and failing to take his mind someplace else, anyplace else. Ilidio's hand went to the generator switch.

"Wait, wait," he said. "There was a diary from Mateus's grandfather. I haven't read it, sir. Mateus said it described battles and had personal stuff too." He paused. "There was a map in the diary." Ilidio's eyes narrowed, and his mouth turn up in a crooked smile.

"I have no idea what was in the map. Seriously, I never saw it!" Another jolt snapped his head back, and he jerked and shook. It stopped, and Tay knew he was in trouble. That was all he had. The next jolt seemed to go on forever.

When Tay came to his senses, Ilidio was gone. His two guards sat bored in their metal chairs, the heat of the afternoon sweltering in the small space. Slumped and shivering, blood and snot trickling down his chin to patter on the filthy floor, Tay stared unseeing at his own reflection in the murky puddle.

Tay thought again about dialing Muni and tried to get his hands loose, but it was no use. The restraints were biting into his skin. His eyes closed, and he dozed, weak from loss of blood and the torture.

Tay awoke later as the world around him seemed to erupt. Gunfire. Chaos. Panic. One guard running outside. It was all a beautiful thing to Tay, and he sat up, hopeful for what would come next.

The last guard stood and peered out the window, gun shaking slightly in hand. A massive, glass shattering explosion from outside knocked him trembling to the ground. Tay's chair rattled and almost pitched him to the floor. His retinas seemed to scream as a bright light flooded the room.

CHAPTER 27
A RESCUE & A KISS

Luanda, Angola, December 14, 2009

Mateus hit the door at a dead run, and it shattered inward. A blood-streaked Mateus rushed in, clenching an aluminum bat in white-knuckled hands. An avenging angel. Warrior saint. Savior. He cast a quick glance at Tay tied up in the chair and stopped cold at the sight.

"What took you so long, Matty?" Tay croaked, his swollen lips and parched tongue making the words little more than a dry whisper. Mateus stumbled but recovered and ran with shaky legs to the front door of the outbuilding, Romiana close behind.

Mateus forced his attention to the guard on the floor. He swung the baseball bat, starting from too far away and in his fury managing to miss, his momentum pivoting him around and down on one knee.

They rose together, Mateus and the guard both struggling to stand. A desperate, overhead ax-like swing with the bat connected with the top of the guard's head. The guard went down, and Mateus followed up with blow after blow to make sure he was not rising anytime soon.

Mateus looked at Tay. He sat there, face a ruin of mottled bruises and crusted blood, one eye swollen shut. His shirt was caked in blood, the ropes were cruelly biting into swollen skin. There was no way he was walking out of here on his own. Eyes rising from his chest, Tay looked up, his weak grin the most beautiful thing Mateus had ever seen. He was alive!

Their eyes met, and something passed between them in that special moment that forged their friendship even deeper. Mateus absorbed the weight of Tay's ordeal, while Tay found solace in the realization that he had not been forsaken. They spoke quietly for a moment.

"What are you doing? *Vamos!*" Romiana burst into the room. "The guards will recover soon. Let's get out of here!" She went to Tay, nimble fingers untying the cruel knots.

Hysterical strength. Mateus knew all about it, people lifting cars in stressful situations, pumped up on adrenaline. Whatever it was, he easily lifted Tay, and they staggered out into the blood-soaked night. Cradling the body of his best friend, Mateus felt reborn, a man of action, of purpose, of resolve.

He looked around and saw the unbelievable destruction. A Empresa guards sprawled on the ground. Fires everywhere among twisted metal. Two bay doors of the warehouse blown inwards. Smoking overturned cars.

Along with Tomé, they were through the fence and sped off into the night in her old sedan, his friends heading off in the old Ford. Tay looked pale and had lost a lot of blood. He needed a doctor.

Romiana said, "I know a Cuban doctor who works with A Empresa sometimes . . . off the record. He's our best shot. I'm not sure at all that he'll help us."

"Get us there. Hurry, Romiana," Mateus pleaded.

They drove the short distance to Luanda Sul, in the southern part of the city, arriving at a complex called Paraiso Condominiums, a wealthy, gated community with guards at the entrance. An unusually diverse community of Angolan, South African, and US expats enjoyed the luxurious homes and manicured gardens.

Romiana spoke in rapid Portuguese to the front-gate guard. While she called him '*Chefe*', an honorific in the city, there was no mistaking the steel in her voice. It was commanding, and the guard responded instantly. He lifted the gate, and they drove inside.

They could see two late model black SUVs in the doctor's driveway, a large screen TV visible in the front window. The front door opened to a tall man with pinched features and an Errol Flynn mustache, answering Romiana's frantic knock. He didn't look happy. Frowning, he said, "*Sí?*"

Romiana used the same assertive tone as with the front gate guard in explaining what they needed. Long before she finished the explanation, the Cuban doctor was shaking his head emphatically and saying, "No. No. No, *señora*." Romiana hesitated. The doctor was closing the front door.

Mateus stepped forward, eyes blazing with unyielding determination, and put his hand firmly against the door. Drawing himself up to his full height, he looked the doctor straight in the eye. The intensity of his gaze made the doctor take a step back.

In flawless Portuguese, Mateus said, "My name is Mateus José Fernando de Silva. I'm the grandson of Premier Coronel Juan Antonio Mateus de Silva. He was a hero of the Revolutionary Army in Angola, and a friend of Fidel Castro." The Cuban doctor froze, expression unreadable. "My friend, my brother, is bleeding out on your doorstep. Your duty is to help our comrade. Your job is clear. You cannot fail the revolution." Romiana looked on in surprise and affection.

One heartbeat. Two. The doctor met Mateus's incendiary gaze. He sighed, looking up and down the quiet street, a hint of fear in his eyes. "Bring in the patient."

Tomé carried an unconscious Tay inside. They lay him on a medical bed in the side room. Dressed in white, the doctor's petite wife emerged, prepared to assist. The doctor stripped off Tay's shirt and went to work, his wife bringing a plasma IV.

All of them jumped when Romiana's phone suddenly trilled. She went outside and onto the front porch, Mateus and Tomé following. A very unhappy Horátio Ilidio was on the line.

Shouting and enraged bellows rang out like gunshots from Romiana's phone. Mateus could see Romiana's shoulders sagging as he cursed her. She started to speak, but he'd already hung up. She appeared dejected, with her eyes fixed on the far distance.

"He knows," she murmured, voice leaden. "About the rescue, the warehouse, all of it. We are to be hunted. There's nowhere in this city we can hide."

Tomé nodded grimly, already fishing for the car keys. "I'll ditch the ride, find us something low-profile. Lie low and stay safe."

As the taillights of the sedan faded into the gloom, Mateus turned to face the woman who had risked everything for him—her livelihood, her family, her very life. He reached out and squeezed her hand tenderly, feeling an unfamiliar surge in his heart.

"Romiana," he began, his throat suddenly tight with emotion. "Your father. Who is he, really? What's his name?" Romiana sighed, eyes downcast.

"His name is Horátio Ilidio," Romiana replied. "Once upon a time, he and your grandfather were rivals, enemies." She kicked at a stray pebble and watched it skitter across the pavement. "This treasure, all of it, every piece, was his. Your grandfather took it from him after the battle and scarred up his face. This is personal for him, gnawing away at him like a cancer for years."

Mateus felt his world tilt on its axis, a sickening lurch of perspective that left him reeling. "Why didn't you tell me this before? I deserved to know the truth. We all did."

"It would not have changed what we have done. I promise." She continued. "I do have something else to tell you. It was not an accident that I was there at the airport to pick you up. I went at the behest of my father. I promise that it's the last thing I'll ever do for him."

Romiana's grip tightened around his hand, willing him to believe her. "I'm on your side and doing everything I can. Surely you can see that. From now on, I walk my own path. And I hope to walk it with you."

Something broke within Mateus at these words. He looked tenderly into her eyes. "I believe you."

They fell into each other's arms, lips meeting in desperation and desire. For one perfect moment, the blood and the bullets and the treasure faded far away. Mateus's first kiss was on a Cuban doctor's porch in Luanda, with his best friend on an operating table a few feet away. Despite all of that, he never wanted it to end.

CHAPTER 28
UNHAPPY CONCESSIONAIRE

Luanda, Angola, December 13, 2009

João Vicente, the Sonangol concessionaire, was unhappy, a simmering pot of barely contained rage. Horátio Ilidio was waiting for him, standing perfectly still in front of the concessionaire's large oak desk. Vicente took his time, forcing him to wait and sweat. He looked out the window of his top-floor office in the beautiful Sonangol office building.

This was the best view in Luanda. The harbor and the city skyline were clear and gorgeous from this vantage. Luanda looked fresh and clean from up here, absolutely beautiful.

Built by Brazil's Odebrecht Construction Company, the Sonangol building was new and had scale models of key facilities in the lobby, walls covered with regional art, and the latest technology, including advanced security and smart elevators. It was a showcase for Angola and the power of Sonangol.

The phone rang, and Vicente picked up the line. After listening for a moment, he said, "Listen, you. Sonangol is the Angolan government's national oil company. We manage all the oil and gas production for the country, as well as the foreign oil companies. Tell me again why I can't place this contract exactly where I want it to go?"

He hung up the phone.

Vicente looked up at a large, colorful map on the wall. The four large blocks of offshore acreage he controlled were outlined in bright gold. He approved all activity and contracts for the blocks. It was a powerful position, as there were billions of dollars spent on each block.

BP and Exxon executives waited for Vicente in the lobby. *They can wait,* he thought. They wanted him to approve a new set of contracts valued at eight hundred million dollars. Vicente had done this finely choreographed dance dozens of times. The executives would present their arguments, showing careful financial analysis and rates of return. They would give him well-thought-out business appraisals, strategic benefits for Angola included. He would nod and appear to listen carefully, asking probing questions.

At the end of all this show, he would tell them who the contracts would go to. It had all been worked out. They had made the decision before the foreigners ever came into the room. Their presentation and their arguments, while interesting, would not change the outcome. He smiled to himself, mocking these self-important expats, these Brits and Americans.

Vicente turned to Ilidio, who was still standing, literally with his hat in his hand, looking uncomfortable and out of place. Vicente thought, not for the first time recently, that he looked old. Horátio had been running A Empresa for almost twenty years. They had accomplished a lot together, but perhaps his time had passed. Vicente had been his government contact for the last seven years, receiving a healthy income from the organization's activities. As powerful as A Empresa was, they needed the government to operate.

Vicente said abruptly and with no greeting or preamble, "Well? Where is my share and what is this explosion going to do to our revenue?"

Ilidio swallowed hard, Adam's apple bobbing. He had a well-rehearsed answer to all of this but paused as if in deep thought. Looking back at Vicente, he thought again of how hard the man was to work with, joining a long line of people who thought the same. Everyone in Sonangol, the executives from BP and Exxon, and even his own family, knew Vicente was a real pain in the ass, rude and belligerent, never listening.

"We have the situation well under control, *chefe*. Until we complete the repairs, we are distributing the merchandise to our other warehouses. We will make changes to the distribution system that will—"

"Under control," Vicente interrupted. He slammed his hand so hard on the desk that Ilidio jumped, and several items fell to the ground. Vincente continued, "You call explosions, men killed, and a hostage escaped being under control? This is not the low-profile operation you promised. You're incompetent. Worthless . . . and what is the impact of this on the revenue?"

"Revenue will be off by about thirty percent for the next month and then fifteen percent the next three months after that," Ilidio said. Vicente knew that this was an opportunity for Ilidio to take a bit of his share off the top, claiming that the bombing had shorted the revenue. That was not happening. Vicente would keep this *puta* firmly under his thumb.

Vicente quietly but in a dangerous tone said, "Here's what's happening. My share's not changing. It's staying exactly where it was before the explosion. If my share goes down by one dollar, you're out of a job. *Comprende?*"

"I understand," Ilidio replied. He had to manage this fiasco so that his own profits stayed whole as well. He had been doing this a long time and had some ideas. Ilidio had already started to raise prices on his street merchandise to help cover this mess.

"We'll get through this, and I'll make sure you're not hurt. That will be my top priority."

"And what of my diamonds?" Vicente asked. "What did the prisoner tell us, and is he still alive?"

Ilidio did not like the sound of "my diamonds."

"Oh, the diamonds. Yes, I interrogated the man. I haven't exactly recovered the diamonds, but I'm tracking them. It is—" He paused, about to say "under control" again, but was not sure his nerves or the desk could stand another pounding.

He stammered a bit. "Just need a bit more time. I will get them. Right now, it's best to let them hunt a bit more. Then we strike."

"You had better be right. Now get the hell out of my sight." Vicente waved Ilidio away, not sure even an eight hundred-million-dollar contract award would cheer him up after this. Looking out once more at his fabulous view, he pondered taking over control of A Empresa himself, even while he left the Exxon executives to wait a bit longer.

Back at his largest warehouse in the city, Ilidio paced through the hallways, his thoughts consumed by plans and haunting memories. He had built this crime syndicate up from nothing, with courage and cunning, and a readiness to shed whatever blood was necessary. He thought back to the early days when he had started his new job at the warehouse many years ago.

Despite being handed the job by his father, Carlos, Ilidio had been determined to be the best, determined to not only make his fortune, but to learn the business. He worked long hours, driving himself and his employees. Every week, without fail, he made the reporting phone call to his father.

The hard work paid off with the finances and the factory books showing very positive numbers. Compared to the past, the operation was generating forty percent more revenue. Ilidio was proud of himself, even if his father was too blind to see, or too stiff and unable to compliment him.

Every Friday afternoon he had visitors to the warehouse, two hard-eyed men from A Empresa. Dressed like anyone else on the Luanda streets, the men wore T-shirts, shorts, and flip-flops. A distinguishing feature was the bulge in the pocket of their shorts, the outline of their gangster pistol.

Horátio Ilidio seethed every week as he paid the A Empresa men. He was too afraid to hold back their share. They were ruthless, and he did not need his father to tell him not to mess around with what he owed. Week after week, his insides churned as the cash tithe left his hand. He vowed to make it stop.

One ordinary Friday, he followed the two men secretly after they left his office, pretending to shop at street vendors along the way. The pair stopped at ten businesses. His jaw dropped as he did a mental calculation of the money they collected every week. It looked so easy, so very easy. He needed this. This easy money was the route to being the big man in Luanda.

The following Friday was the day, circled on his calendar in red pen. He had figured that the money the pair collected had to be given to a higher up, the next person on the ladder to the top of A Empresa. He would follow them again.

Ilidio watched side-eyed from a food stall as the men went past AK-47 toting guards and into a tidy, light-blue office building. He could see a second-story window where the men were speaking to someone behind a desk. This was all he needed, a plan taking shape in his ruthless mind.

Late the following Sunday night, Ilidio revisited the office. The single guard at the front door was sitting in a plastic chair and sleeping, head resting on his shoulder. Ilidio hurriedly scurried to the back of the building, a small smile building on his face at his slow heart rate and composure.

With a towel-wrapped brick, he carefully broke out a window, cracking it as quietly as possible. He meticulously took out all the glass to ensure that a casual passerby wouldn't detect anything wrong. Laying the towel over the opening, he crawled through and made his way to the office of the A Empresa boss.

Ilidio set his backpack down. He shoved the Glock into his

waistband and held a vicious-looking steel bar lightly in his right hand. The other items could wait. His mind still, he hummed a silent tune.

At 9:30 a.m. sharp, a small thin man strode into the office, wearing gray knit slacks and a colorful flowery silk shirt. His soft leather loafers made a slight swishing sound as he walked. The man was two steps into the office when his world turned upside down. Ilidio clubbed him in the back of the skull, the iron bar connecting with a thud. The man crumpled to the ground like a sack of rice, while Ilidio calmly shut and locked the office door.

The man woke to an excruciating splitting headache and limbs that were held securely in place. He looked down and saw that he was naked, strapped firmly to the wooden office chair with duct tape that also covered his mouth. He struggled to breathe through the nose, sniffling and snorting for air. As his head cleared, the man was startled to hear someone talking to him.

"Hello, *mi amigo,*" said Ilidio. "You're going to tell me exactly what I need to know, or you will not leave this office alive. Do you understand?" The man nodded vigorously, shoulders bobbing, eager to please. Ilidio shook his head slowly. "Not good enough."

Ilidio swung the iron club. A swishing sound through the air, and a vicious blow that crushed the man's right kneecap. The man saw stars and flashing lights, and he screamed under the tape. His body shook with pain, tears poured from his eyes.

"Do you understand?" The man had not become an A Empresa boss by being dumb. With his knee already swelling, he looked Ilidio directly in the eyes. He slowly and carefully nodded, keeping his eyes on Ilidio.

"Much better," said Ilidio, and promptly bashed the left kneecap. The man's scream was audible even underneath the duct tape. Ilidio took his time, waiting until the man was back under control.

"Listen carefully because I won't ask twice. I need to know everything. You're going to tell me every last detail about the operation. Who makes the deliveries, and on what schedule. Names and ranks of everyone you answer to, and exactly how much they're skimming off the top. Names and positions of all the men at the top of A Empresa. Don't even think about holding back on me."

Ilidio paused and looked the man coldly in the eye. "Lie to me, and you'll be sorry." The man was sweating profusely despite the cool air conditioning in the office. His knees were ballooning, and his naked body trembled with shock.

Duct tape ripped off his mouth, the sound echoing in the office. The man worked his mouth back and forth, wet his lips with his tongue, and began talking. Ilidio listened intently, taking notes on a notepad ready on top of the desk. The man talked, with only a few interrupting questions by Ilidio. There were names, addresses, times, and dates. The man spilled it all, words pouring out, eager to survive this maniac.

Thirty minutes later, Ilidio finished the questioning and sat calmly at the man's desk. He was wearing a tan suit with a pale blue oxford shirt. Cufflinks and a bright paisley pocket square marked him as a stylish and serious man. He reviewed paperwork on the desk and in the filing cabinet while he waited. There were two hours until the first scheduled money drop.

Behind the office closet door, the former syndicate boss lay dead. He had been strangled and stuffed unceremoniously into the closet. Ilidio would dispose of the body later that night.

Two men knocked on his office door precisely on time. "Enter," Ilidio said. The two men stepped in and stopped, confused. They did not see their contact, but instead a professional-looking man with a scary-looking scar on his face.

"Sit down and listen," the former general commanded. The two men sat down quickly.

"I am in charge. You'll report to me from now on. No matter what happens, I get my money. Understand?" The men nodded and looked down. "Understand!" Ilidio yelled.

"Sí, *chefe!*" they both replied.

"Good. We'll work well together. You'll find that I reward the men who serve me well." He smiled without mirth, the brightness of it almost obscuring the dark scar. He pulled out some bills from his wallet. "First, I am buying you suits and white shirts. We're going to make you look the part of a gangster. Next, we will talk about raising your pay." The men looked at one another and smiled cautiously.

That was the start. He was accepted by A Empresa almost immediately, his efficiency and style making him stand out. Ilidio moved up in the organization over time, ruthless moves eliminating or pushing aside rivals and those above him. There were one or two engineered robberies gone wrong, with an A Empresa boss getting killed along the way. There was a mysterious disappearance of another. All were simply stepping stones.

When the head of the entire organization died of an apparent heart attack, it became natural for Ilidio to step into the role. As the head of A Empresa, he expanded its reach and influence to extraordinary heights. He eliminated rival criminal organizations with the same ruthlessness that had pushed him to the top.

Ilidio had to make absolutely sure this concessionaire did not screw it all up. For the first time in his life, he had a grudging acceptance from his father. He was not sure and didn't care if this was from mutual respect or fear. Getting the diamonds was the final piece, the crown jewels, so to speak.

The diamonds would be his, no matter what it took and who he had to kill to get them.

CHAPTER 29
DOCTORED IN PARAISO

Luanda, Angola, December 14, 2009

The first pale fingers of dawn crept through the curtains of the doctor's house in Paraiso Condominium, casting a gentle glow over the sleeping forms of Mateus and Romiana. They'd spent a restless night on the overstuffed couch and chair, their minds awhirl with the events of the past twenty-four hours.

The comforting aroma of eggs and bacon slowly roused them from their sleep. Mateus blinked blearily, neck kinked from the awkward sleeping position. Romiana stretched beside him, her hair tousled and eyes heavy with exhaustion.

Mateus found Tay sitting up and looking much better. The saline drip was doing its work, and his shoulder sported a clean white bandage and sling. Mateus felt his stomach unclench, and said with forced humor, "You still slacking in here, big guy?"

Tay replied, "You know, on Level 32 of *Legends*, where you fall through those blender screws, get chewed up, get hit with RPG shells front and back, and then go directly into the nest of porcupine grenades? That's about how I feel."

Mateus barked a laugh. It had been a while since either had thought about video games, and it was somehow comforting. The dose of fantasy in this incredibly real situation seemed to help. Tay's grin faded, and his eyes turned serious.

"I saw what you did back there, Matty. Charging in like some action hero. I don't know how to thank you, man." Mateus swallowed hard, but Tay's twinkling smile returned. "By the way, who are you, and what've you done with Mateus?"

"It's been a journey, and we're not there yet," said Mateus. He settled into the chair beside Tay's bed, filling him in on all that had transpired. Despite his photographic memory, he managed to leave out the passionate kiss with Romiana.

As the first rays of sunset painted the sky in orange and red fire, the companions prepared to make their escape, thanking the doctor and his wife profusely. Tay, stubborn as ever, insisted on walking under his own power, even as he leaned heavily on Mateus for support.

Romiana and Tomé had spent the day securing supplies food, water, medical necessities, and other supplies, and had scouted potential safe houses. In the end, they settled on the half-finished construction site where they'd first hatched their rescue plan. It was remote, defensible, and far from the prying eyes of Horátio Ilidio's goons.

They huddled around the makeshift table, a single bare bulb throwing their shadows onto unfinished walls. The gravity of what they were facing hit them all like a leaden weight.

"Tay, with your injury and the real and present danger, we're out of here, back to Los Angeles. We get out while we're still alive. Get out before we pick up any more bullet holes." said Mateus.

Romiana knit her brows and slightly shook her head. The idea of Mateus leaving on a plane was clearly painful.

Tay's jaw clenched, a stubborn set to his shoulders. "I'm not running, Matty. Not now, not ever. We started this thing together, and that's how we're gonna finish it."

"No way. This is too big a gamble and too big a risk. Let's get out of here."

"I'm not going anywhere. Let's hear the plan." Tay's face brooked no argument, and he clearly expected Mateus to have already developed the plan.

Mateus sighed, eyes momentarily downward, then into Tay's eyes and Romiana's. He reached for his grandfather's journal, the leather cover supple and warm beneath his fingertips. He'd pored over the faded pages, committing every word and every sketch to memory.

"Tundavala," he whispered. "That's where we're going. My grandfather's journal spelled it out. Clear-cut instructions. An unmistakable map. No cryptic poems or riddles to deal with. Simple."

"Nothing is going to be simple," said Romiana. "We are on a death list with my father and his A Empresa. We can't move around the city or the country like we used to. It's way too risky. We'll need to be extremely careful and very lucky if we want to stay alive."

"I get it. This is still going to be a big challenge even with the map."

"It gets worse. A Empresa has extensive government connections. I'm not convinced that you'll be able to leave the country without getting caught and thrown in jail." Romiana knew her father sent vast sums of money to highly placed government officials. This allowed him to call in favors for situations like this, situations where interests aligned.

"Our best bet is to maintain a very low-profile," said Romiana. "We can't let ourselves be seen. The word will be out, and a reward put on all our heads. Slowly, slowly is the way."

Mateus jabbed a finger at the weathered pages, eyes alight with manic energy. "But first, we need to get Tay healthy. We're not going to risk his health for any treasure in the world." He paused for several heartbeats. "Next, we call on our secret weapon, Muni, the drone wizard. We need her to lay a false trail, to make Ilidio think we're running north to the Congo. Electronic breadcrumbs, ghosts in the machine." Romiana and Tay both nodded. "Finally, we move. We are heading south, my friends, south to Lubango, south to Tundavala Gap. For the treasure is sitting there, waiting for us."

A sense of grim purpose settled over the safe house. They stood and clasped hands, gazing at one another, united in this thing together.

CHAPTER 30
BLOODY HANDS

Lubango, Angola, January 9, 1984

The oppressive heat of the St. Joseph Cathedral bore down on Colonel Juan de Silva like a physical weight, scents of sweat and incense thick in his nostrils. Still, he sat ramrod straight in the crowded pew as the priest intoned the mass. In contrast to those in threadbare clothes around him, the colonel sat in starched fatigues with knife-edge pleats, every inch the military officer.

De Silva paid close attention to the liturgy despite his intentions. Today was a day of reflection, a final atonement before his act of sacrilege and the helicopter likely taking him to his death.

Tomorrow, he would be whisked away to the front lines, to Cuanza Sul, where the specter of death awaited. De Silva's gaze drifted to the backpack at his feet, its nondescript exterior belying the fortune concealed within. Seventy pounds of rough diamonds. Today was his last chance to hide the diamonds, his last chance to provide a legacy to the family that he had neglected for the sake of Cuba and his military career.

De Silva looked up as the priest intoned The Profession of Faith, *"Creio em um só Deus, Pai todo-poderoso, Criador do céu e da terra."* He saw the two Angolan altar boys with their brilliant, pristine white robes and scrubbed faces. De Silva's thoughts drifted from the liturgy to his own childhood, when he was a young altar boy in Santo Domingo.

Evening Mass over, de Silva stayed behind, head bowed in the pew. As the crowd filtered outside, no one took notice of him or the backpack at his feet. It seemed natural for a soldier to have such a thing. It was not natural for a soldier to be carrying a fortune in the middle of the Lubango cathedral.

De Silva rose slowly and went to the cleaning closet at the rear of the sanctuary, retrieving a hammer, chisel, putty knife, trowel, and mortar, all hidden previously. He prayed in earnest, looking around the humble cathedral with plain white walls and a concrete floor, the ceiling with white painted structural beams supporting a corrugated roof. He looked to the front of the church, at a simple brown cross with the cursive Portuguese words, *Father, forgive them for they know not what they do.* To the right of the altar, he saw a plinth supporting a life-sized statue of the Virgin Mary.

The pedestal had a white cloth edged with embroidered pink and blue flowers on a lace background. Mary was colorful, with a bright blue cloak flowing around her body. A white shawl covered her head and flowing brown hair. She had a calm expression that seemed to exude motherly love.

De Silva sat still in the plastic chair, looking at the statue and thinking of the Cuban revolution. He had dedicated his life to his country and to the cause, and they did this to him, gave him Dolores, a bastard daughter. While the diamonds would provide a significant boost to the cause, De Silva was reluctant to hand them over to Cuba. This treasure was for his family. After what they did to him, duty was no longer the priority.

The cathedral was empty, and the sun was low in the sky. De Silva was nervous and unwilling to move forward. He prayed anxiously, sweat pouring from his face and hands. His eyes opened, and his hands were slick with blood, crimson rivulets, like some macabre stigmata. He blinked furiously, heart pounding in his chest. When he looked again, the vision had passed, and his hands were back to normal. Looking up, he could see the obscene trick of the light, sunset coursing through red stained glass. *Pull yourself together, de Silva,* he thought.

Finally, he stood, looking up at the Virgin Mary, who gazed back at him with serene, peaceful eyes. "Forgive me, Mother," he whispered, his voice hoarse with emotion. "For what I am about to do."

CHAPTER 31
TEN BAGS

Luanda, Angola, January 14, 2010

Mateus felt a surge of joy as the crackling static of the phone fed him Muni's familiar voice. It was a taste of home, which right now felt very far away. She was so amazing, this eye in the sky, infiltrating hacker, army of one.

"A false trail," she mused, the faint clicking of keys underscoring her words. "Breadcrumbs in the digital ether, leading your hunters on a merry chase to the north. Yes." More clicking. "Yes, I think I can manage that. It would be good for you to send me details for all of you. ID. Credit cards. Pictures. We need to paint a picture of all of you together, my little hobbits, to fool those nasty orcs."

Muni's mind whirled. CCTV images. Receipts at gas stations and restaurants. The *pièce de resistance*, documentation of them crossing the border over into the Congo. She smiled. This would keep their enemies busy for some time.

Muni hoped privately that this would not trigger a war. Crashing an Israeli drone and exploding it in the middle of a capital city came pretty close to an international incident. Mateus interrupted her thinking.

"You're a lifesaver, my Gandalf. Literally. Thanks so much." As Mateus clicked off, he felt a surge of pleasure and something akin to contentment. He had Muni to bounce ideas off of while Tay recovered from his gunshot. She was great for that. It seemed like his grandfather's de Silva's planning gene had somehow kicked in suddenly, and he was thinking about contingency plans, trying to stay ahead of the next events and A Empresa.

The sun was down as they prepared to leave, the star-lit Luanda sky a glittering marvel. Tomé had been busy getting food, a new vehicle, and more antibiotics for Tay. He seemed to be excited about the trip, and it showed on his face and demeanor.

The drive to Lubango was a blur. Fifteen hours of dusty roads were punctuated by a single, fitful night in a ramshackle hotel in the laidback coastal city of Lobito. Tay dozed uneasily in the backseat while Romiana and Tomé took turns driving. Even as the miles fell away beneath their tires, Mateus could not shake a growing feeling of dread. The specter of Horátio Ilidio's vengeance loomed large in his mind, a shadow that lengthened with each passing hour.

In their excitement, they drove immediately to St. Joseph's Cathedral. The two spires of the church were backlit by the sun. Thin crosses, adorned with slender rings at the top of each spire, threw off long shadows reaching toward them. An empty kidney-shaped fountain in the church courtyard, its blue tiles cracking.

Mateus missed all of this, his nerves strung tight as piano wire. All he could see was the ghost of his grandfather walking in this very courtyard. The colonel seemed to still be in this place, behind every corner and in every soft breeze. Juan de Silva, the war hero, his grandfather, the man who had set them all on this stormy path.

Tay had healed quickly and was moving well, his arm in a sling but otherwise seemingly healthy. They wandered for a time through the people in the streets around the church. Mateus took in the now familiar scenes of Angolan life—the buying and selling of food, conversation and laughing, mothers carrying babies on their backs or on their laps. The flamboyant taxi drivers seemed to be everywhere, trying to attract him, first with their words and then sometimes by grabbing his arm and pulling.

Mateus watched the joy in the conversations and their care and love of children. These people had next to nothing, but they were living life and engaging with one another, smiling always. This Cal Tech guy who hated travel, with gangsters trying to kill him, was glad for a moment that he was here.

The St. Joseph's Cathedral was locked, but mass was starting soon. They found a shady spot near the fountain and settled in to wait.

"The cathedral's not Notre Dame, but it has a simple beauty, eh?" said Tay.

Mateus replied, "Agreed. The cathedral must have looked the same to my grandfather, but maybe this fountain was flowing. The Tundavala Gap is over those hills to the northeast about fifteen miles. He had a tremendous victory there, commanding a large army. But now, it's time for mass."

The priest's voice boomed out in the simple cathedral, bouncing off the bare structural ceiling beams. He spoke confidently, his bald head and clean white frock giving him a devout air. Mateus and Tay took part fully, kneeling and praying with the congregation. They took the Eucharist from the priest's hand, solemnly placing it in their mouths. Tay felt a bit of guilt but rationalized his participation—the Baptist guy in strange territory. *When in Rome . . .*

Mateus looked carefully at the Madonna. She gazed back serenely and seemed to encourage him. At least, that is what he imagined. The map showed the treasure to be right under her.

As darkness fell and the streets emptied of life, Mateus led the squad through the shadows, the foursome moving as one. There were no cars out at this late hour, and it was quiet. Mateus could hear the quiet crunch of the gravel beneath their shoes. Bolt cutters made quick work of the rusted locks, and they were inside the courtyard.

Romiana watched him, her dark eyes sparkling with intensity and concentration.

"It's going to be okay," he whispered. She nodded and squeezed his bicep. For the first time in his life, he wished they were bigger. Maybe he should have spent more time in the gym.

Tomé was resourceful, having gathered an array of bolt cutters, lock picks, hammers, chisels, mortar, and trowels. There were a couple of headlamps and two shovels. All that was missing for them to be on a construction squad were hard hats and steel-toed shoes. The night was chilly, and the air felt clean in their lungs.

Mateus's plan was simple. Romiana would remain at the door on lookout while Mateus and Tomé moved the statue. Mateus would excavate the plinth and hopefully uncover the diamonds. Tay would work to keep the site clean while the digging was ongoing.

The cathedral was quiet as a tomb, with heavy, incense-flavored air wafting over them like a blanket. Long shadows from the meager light of the small windows fell around them, dark arms reaching out. The words under the cross were visible, *Father, forgive them, for they know not what they do*. Mateus shivered and hoped these words were not prophetic.

His eyes were drawn to the statue of the Virgin Mary, her serene gaze following him as he moved through the gloom. Calm, patient eyes. Blue cape wrapped around her body. White dress. She seemed somehow alive. On impulse, Mateus sank to his knees and prayed. Romiana quickly followed suit, and the two of them were together on the cathedral floor.

Tay watched with interest, his Southern Baptist roots giving him a different view of kneeling before Mary. Tomé watched but did not kneel. He shifted from one foot to the other, looking uncomfortable.

Mateus called Muni. "Hey, I'm looking at Mary's plinth. It's about three and a half feet tall and covered in a white, laced cloth."

"Keep me on the line," said Muni.

Mateus crossed himself and grabbed the statue around her knees.

He tugged. Nothing happened. He braced his legs against the plinth and leaned backward with all his strength, almost willing the statue to move.

Mary shifted slowly at first and then sped up right to the edge of the plinth, threatening to fall. The white cloth had moved and was bunching around his ankles. He caught his breath and readied himself for the final lift, steadying Mary and banishing thoughts of her in pieces on the floor. Mateus and Tomé lifted and set her gently down on the concrete floor.

Mateus rapped on the plinth with his knuckles, assuming that it was made of concrete masonry bricks like most buildings and structures in Angola. There was plenty of room inside to use as a hiding place for the Tundavala treasure.

In the moonlight, they could see that someone had redone the top surface of the plinth. Mateus looked into Romiana's eyes with a big smile. Romiana smiled back.

Mateus's headlamp shone brightly, focusing as he got to work on the top of the plinth. The chisel bit into the plaster with a crunch, chips of stone and mortar pattering to the floor like hailstones. He used a rag over the top of the chisel to keep his exertions quieter. The top layer of stucco came away quickly with each chisel strike, revealing the concrete bricks below.

He tried to keep the disappointment from his face and actions. The childlike portion of his brain expected diamonds to come streaming out of the top of the plinth, perhaps accompanied by rainbows and unicorns. The reality was that he had some excavation work to do. He and Tomé had an urgent whispered conversation, and Mateus was reassured. They needed to go deeper.

The chisel bit into the mortar between the concrete bricks. Chips were flying, with both mortar and the bricks themselves disintegrating. There was a fair bit of noise, and he stopped to look over at Romiana by the door. She gave him the thumbs up, and he continued.

Sweating, he could pry what remained of two bricks from the top layer with the crowbar. Two more bricks came loose, and he lifted them out, revealing a hidden chamber within.

Mateus's heart leaped as he thrust his hand into the opening, his fingers closing around the rough canvas of a heavy bag. He withdrew it slowly, reverently, scarcely daring to breathe.

His headlamp revealed stenciled letters with the word *UNITA* across the bag. His knees shook as he grabbed the plinth to steady himself. Even after the poems and the maps and cigar boxes and car chases, there was a part of him that believed there would be nothing here. But this was absolutely real. The bag was heavy at about six or seven pounds. His grandfather had placed it under Mary, just for him.

Romiana ran over and was by his side. They all stared at the bag, momentarily frozen. With trembling hands, Mateus gently upended the bag onto a nearby chair.

A cascade of diamonds spilled out, freed from the darkness of the bag. It was as if they had been saving up all of their sparkling for this moment. Their facets caught the meager light and threw it back, glittering and shining, dazzling and flashing, as if brightness were bursting from their hearts.

For a long moment, the four of them simply stared in wonder, transfixed, frozen. A king's ransom. A fortune. This was truly a treasure.

Mateus carefully placed each diamond back in the bag. "Listen, we will have plenty of time to look at these later. We need to get the diamonds out of the hole and get Mary back up on that plinth." They nodded. Tay put the bag into the large canvas duffel they had brought for this purpose.

Mateus moved quickly to the plinth, his breathing loud from excitement, and carefully plucked out nine more bags. They were identical to the first, around seven pounds each, and marked with a *UNITA* stencil.

Mateus's thoughts turned to his grandfather as he handed each bag to Tay. His grandfather had been right here and had hidden these under the Virgin. He wished that he could have known him. The last bag was out of the plinth and into the duffel. He flashed his headlamp all around the inside and looked carefully, to be sure.

Mateus said, "Okay, that's it. Let's close this up and get out of here." No one replied. Tay was looking past him, eyes widened in shock. A sudden sound from behind froze him in his tracks. A familiar metallic click. Unmistakable. Chilling.

Mateus whirled around, dread rising in his gut. There he was. Tomé. Standing like a menacing sentinel. Body coiled in a combat stance. Arms extended. Finger on trigger. The barrel of his massive revolver was leveled at Mateus's head, steady and unwavering with lethal malice.

CHAPTER 32
BETRAYAL

Lubango, Angola, January 17, 2010

The air in the cathedral crackled with tension as Mateus stared down the barrel of Tomé's gun, the cold steel glinting in the faint light. "Don't move," Tomé growled, his voice echoing through the sacred space. Then louder, "Alright, come in!"

Romiana's eyes widened. "Tomé," she whispered, her voice thick with hurt and disbelief.

The doors at the rear of the cathedral swung open, revealing three figures striding purposefully down the aisle. In the center, an older man with a jagged scar on his face, flanked by two suited enforcers. Horátio Ilidio grinned with satisfaction as he drank in the scene before him.

Tay swayed on his feet, his breath catching as he locked eyes with his former tormentor. Mateus stepped in front of Tay protectively, squaring his shoulders as he met Ilidio's gaze unflinchingly. Two A Empresa goons pointed their guns aggressively at Mateus's chest.

"Thank you for recovering my diamonds," Ilidio crowed with a sinister grin. "It's been far too long since I last saw them." He jabbed a finger at his ruined cheek. "Your grandfather gave me this, boy. And then he robbed me of my diamonds."

Mateus's jaw clenched, fire in his eyes. "He also totally defeated you in the battle at Tundavala." Ilidio grin turned steely. "These diamonds belonged to UNITA, not to you. You lost the war. The UNITA army is no more. They're not your diamonds. They're our diamonds." Mateus stood with fists clenched, as if this was somehow a match for the weapons arrayed against them. Tay straightened, and Romiana reached down slowly to wrap her hand around the crowbar.

Ilidio erupted into laughter, and even the two stern-faced guards smiled. "Let's be reasonable, my friends. No one has to get hurt. Hand over the stones, and you can walk away with your lives."

Romiana shook her head vehemently. "Don't trust him," she warned.

Ilidio rounded on her, face contorting with rage. "Traitor!" he spat, flecks of spittle flying from his lips. "*Puta!* First, you stop reporting on these fools, and now you turn your back on your own flesh and blood?" Ilidio's face flushed with fury.

"In Angola, we respect our elders. We honor our fathers here. But you, you're no child of mine. Not anymore." Ilidio turned to his black-suited guards. "Kill her and the Black one. Leave the tall one for me."

As he finished speaking, chaos erupted around them. Cell phones came to life in a cacophony of sounds and vibration. The cathedral filled with unruly noise. Latin music. Tinny ring tones. Portuguese rap music. Bells. Beeps. All accompanied by phone pulsations in pockets.

Eyes widened in surprise when the fire alarm abruptly shrieked, its piercing noise accompanied by pulsating red and white emergency lights. Without pause, the sprinkler system activated and drenched the stunned assembly.

It was Muni, of course, their contingency plan, listening in and waiting for just the right moment to unleash her digital hurricane. She smiled as she listened in on the sounds and confusion. It was not crashing an Israeli drone into a warehouse, but it was still fun.

Ilidio's guards fumbled for ringing phones, put their hands over their ears against the fire alarm, and shielded their eyes from the sprinkler downpour.

The tomb raiding trio sprang into action. Romiana lunged, her crowbar carving a smooth arc through the air before crashing into the temple of the nearest guard. Teeth and blood sprayed onto the cathedral floor, and he buckled to the ground.

Tay, one arm in a sling from his gunshot, lurched forward as his years of martial arts training triggered. Muscle memory and skill. He sprinted two steps and launched his body into the air, spinning to catch the second enforcer with a devastating kick to the face. The guard's nose crumpled, head snapping back. Before he fell, Tay pivoted and kicked him once more to the other side of the head. The guard was down and out, eyes rolling to the back of his head.

"Okay, Muni, enough," Mateus said. Instantly, the cell phones fell silent, and the fire alarm was silenced. The water from the sprinklers slowed to a mere trickle. Mateus reached calmly into the duffel bag and pulled out a Glock pistol, aiming it at the center of Ilidio's chest.

Mateus had suspected that something might go wrong in this cathedral. A Empresa had a long reach, and he had thought that somehow they might catch up to them, despite the electronic breadcrumbs that drew their attention north.

And Tomé. It seemed too easy for him to get guns and gunmen. An uncanny ease that even included obtaining stolen cars. A Empresa controlled the city, and it seemed even to an American like Mateus, that it would be hard to do all that without their knowledge. Mateus had tried to think and act like his warrior grandfather.

Tay was grinning. "So, mastermind. All those contingency meetings with Muni. Hiding the gun in the duffel bag. You were right. It worked!"

"Operation Battle of the Black Gate was a success!" came Muni's voice over the phone, the obscure Tolkien reference lost on Romiana.

"I think you all have forgotten about me," said Ilidio, smugly. Aged and soaking wet, unarmed and standing between two unconscious guards, Mateus thought he still somehow looked and sounded every bit the head of the leading crime syndicate in Angola.

Ilidio smiled and seemed relaxed, even with Mateus's gun pointed at him. "The other thing you've forgotten, my little general," he said, "is that behind you is my Tomé. Behind you is my man. He has a gun pointed at your two friends. Now drop your weapon or watch them die."

Mateus looked amused, as if about to show a winning poker hand. "That would seem to be a problem. Tay, could you do me a favor and take that gun off his hands? If he makes things difficult, kick the side of his head in."

"With pleasure."

"Shoot them! Kill them all!" Ilidio roared, eyes bulging and spit flying from his lips.

Tomé was nothing if not obedient. He thrust his hand out, aimed the .38-special caliber revolver at Tay, and started rapidly pulling the trigger. Once. Twice. Three times. Nothing happened. Tomé's eyes went down, confusion on his face. He knew the gun was loaded and the cylinder had rotated. But nothing. "What the . . ." Tomé frowned and took a step back.

"The gun won't fire," said Tay, grinning as he pulled a small file from his pocket. He waved it in front of Tomé and took a step forward with his one good fist raised. "My best friend is a general who thinks of everything, and you are in deep shit, dude. I filed down the firing pin on that while you were asleep." He pointed to the pistol. "It's just a hunk of metal now." Tay took a menacing step toward the man.

Tomé had seen enough. He'd grown up on the streets of Angola, fending for himself. His history made him very proficient in reading situations, instantly calculating odds, and reacting based on the result. He turned and ran, not stopping to look back or get permission from his boss. Ilidio watched, incredulity and rage clear on his craggy features.

"Looks like it's just us left," Mateus said to Ilidio, the aim of his pistol never wavering. His mind raced as he thought of their options.

The military man, his grandfather, would simply kill Ilidio and make a quick getaway. Smart but callous. Mateus could not bring himself to kill a man in cold blood, no matter how heinous. Even though he knew that if positions were reversed, his life would be over. Mateus looked over at Romiana.

"We have to get out of here. What should we do with him?"

Romiana met his gaze, eyes hard as flint. "Options are to kill him or take him with us. The safest bet is to kill him, eliminate the threat. I think that—"

"Wait, wait, wait, hold on here," Ilidio interrupted, his voice cracking with desperation. "You don't need to do that. I can still help you. I can guarantee you safe passage out of the country. We can come to an arrangement. I give you my word."

Mateus hesitated, unsure and untrusting.

Tay jumped in. "Matty, we need to move, *hermano*. Whatever you're going to do, do it now." They weren't hearing sirens, but even a passing car could be trouble at this point.

Mateus nodded, body straightening in resolve. This man had tortured his friend and planned to kill them all in this holy place. In a fluid motion, he aimed and squeezed the trigger.

The shot rang out like thunder, and Ilidio staggered back, clutching at his left shoulder, exactly the spot where Tay was hit. A red plume appeared, and Ilidio went down gasping. Mateus had a momentary good feeling, karma fulfilled, even as a premonition of dark futures washed over him. Despite the wound, Mateus feared they had not seen the last of Generalissimo Horátio Ilidio.

"We're outta here!" he said, pushing the gun back into the duffel bag.

With a grunt and a heave of the diamond-laden sack over his back, they were moving. Mateus looked back at the statue of the Virgin, now sitting on the floor. Crossing himself, he said, "I'm so sorry, Mother Mary." Getting her safely back on the plinth was not an option.

"Muni, can you still hear me?"

"I'm here." The cell phone connection was still intact.

"Please get an ambulance on the way to the cathedral. I wanted to wound this man, not kill him."

"I'm on it," she said.

They were outside. The cool air felt refreshing against their skin, despite the chill from their wet clothes. Duffel bag in the trunk, they clicked their seatbelts and sped off into the night, tires squealing yet again.

Ilidio heard the car moving away, his shoulder on fire. He started dialing his cell phone, blood running down his arm and onto the keys. Phone calls made, Ilidio lay still, cursing under his breath, pressing the rag hard into his shoulder.

"Twice! The diamonds should have been in my hand twice now!" Ilidio talked to himself with eyes narrowed in pain. "If that *cabrão* Tomé hadn't let them disable his gun, this would be all over even with all the computer witchcraft. Shit. Shit. Shit!"

Lying on the cold, hard floor of St. Joseph's Cathedral in Lubango, a bullet lodged in his shoulder, Ilidio, the disgraced general and gangster head, made a solemn vow in this holy place. He would employ every ounce of his cunning, leverage every resource, and let nothing stand in his way. Ilidio would destroy both Mateus and his traitorous daughter, Romiana.

He would show his father, Carlos. He would show them all. The diamonds would be his. Nothing would stop him.

CHAPTER 33
DIAMOND FEVER

Lubango, Angola, January 17, 2010

Mateus, Tay, and Romiana huddled on the dirt floor of an abandoned building in Lubango, their eyes wide and hearts pounding. Between them sat a heavy, lumpy duffel bag holding a treasure trove they were now ready to fully inspect. They had only gotten a glimpse of what the bags held when in the dark cathedral.

"Wait," Mateus whispered, stalling for time and fumbling for his phone. "Muni should be here for this. She's earned it, that wizard." Tay and Romiana nodded, their faces taut with barely contained excitement.

"We want you to be here with us for the grand unveiling," Mateus said into the phone.

"Alright, my intrepid hobbits," Muni chirped, her smile lighting up the screen. "Let's do this. Smaug's treasure!"

Her words broke the stalemate, and they were suddenly excited and ready to dig in. Mateus unzipped the duffel bag while Tay smiled and overdramatically started singing the theme from *Jaws*, "Duuun dun . . . duuun dun . . . dun dun dun dun dun dun . . ."

Mateus's fist closed around the first of the ten bags. Dark green canvas labeled with black stenciled *UNITA* on the side. It was heavy, about the size of a football. He resisted the temptation to give it a little toss in the air. Mateus opened the bag and poured the contents onto a ratty towel. The diamonds came tumbling out, tinkling and clicking together. He emptied the entire bag.

Even seeing them for the second time, their mouths were wide, jaws dropping open. For a long moment, they stared in mute wonder, transfixed. Even though they were rough and uncut, the diamonds were spectacular. The sparkling mound glittered and popped with color and vibrancy, a thousand stars winking and dancing in the sun. The pile remained still, while the light danced between the stones, shimmering in some places and gleaming brightly in others.

Mateus had studied diamonds to prepare for this moment, his brain in overdrive.

"Close to thirty carats. A typically high refractive index," he mumbled, holding a larger stone up to the bright Angolan sun. "Optimal critical angle for total internal reflection. Colorless with no inclusions. Hmm . . . good."

"How romantic, professor," said Romiana dryly, reaching for a diamond herself in wonder.

Mateus looked at her fondly. He loved the way her face looked, bright eyes shining with excitement, a beautiful smile. Could she be a part of that future? He wanted her beside him, in his life, and his bed. Commitment was a scary idea, but he thought anyway of their future and their kids, running around the house and playing in the backyard.

"Earth to Mateus! Tell us what you are thinking," Tay said, not surprised, as he'd seen Mateus drift off many times.

Mateus snapped back to the present. Shaking his head to clear it, he continued in a louder voice.

"These look to be gem grade. Cut and clarity are outstanding. Even without a jeweler's loupe, I can tell you that these are exceptional. The sizes are incredible. This one, for example." He held up the one in his hand. "This is about a thirty-carat stone. It's pink, which makes it very rare. It looks like a gemologist grade D, which is the best. This single stone, by itself, even uncut, is worth over ten million."

As that sunk in, Mateus continued. "I would estimate that this bag is worth fifty-to-sixty million by itself. If this is representative of the other bags, we have just recovered a three hundred-to-four hundred-million-dollar treasure."

There was a tinny "Woo hoo!" from Muni on the phone.

Tay exclaimed, "Woah!" He picked up another large one and held it to the light. Romiana did the same. All three became somewhat hypnotized. Time passed as they examined diamond after diamond. Far from getting bored, each new stone seemed to be unique and held its own unique spark and flash.

Muni waited for a while patiently. Finally, she said, "Guys, we may want to think some about the other nine bags and the criminals who're trying to kill you."

Romiana nodded. "This smart woman speaks the truth. Let's go."

Opening the other bags, they spent the next few minutes methodically ensuring that they all contained diamonds. They saw the stones in each fresh bag were nicer than the previous one. Reluctantly, they returned the stones to the duffel bag.

"We need to focus, guys," Mateus said almost reluctantly. "First, we need to get to a safe place and get valid traveling documents. Second, we need to get out of Angola. Third, we will need to have a plan for transporting the diamonds."

Mateus looked from Tay to Romiana and back. They seemed to be with him. "Finally, we need to figure out how to sell the diamonds. That area can wait. Let's talk about number one, getting ourselves safe and traveling. Romiana, what do you think?" Unspoken in his mind but of utmost importance was whether she was going with them.

"A Empresa will have eyes at every airport, train station, and border crossing across Angola. We'll need to get creative if we want to slip the net. They will have our names and descriptions. Dedicated teams will search for us, focusing on train and air terminals, but also on the streets. They will go all out."

She continued, her mouth set and gaze serious. "It's likely that some of those teams are already active in Lubango. We found the treasure, but we're in danger. I don't need to tell any of you how serious this is. They'll kill us if it gets them the diamonds, or even just for revenge at this point."

Mateus looked at the ground and said quietly, "You're coming with us?"

Romiana looked at him with big eyes and said simply, "Yes." Mateus squeezed her hand briefly and then it was back to business.

Romiana added, "Tay should drive, if he can do that with one hand. They'll be looking for me in the driver's seat. I'll be in the passenger seat and Mateus. You'll lie down in the back seat. Observers will see an African male driver, a female passenger, and that's all. We also need new clothes."

"I can drive." Tay smiled. "Mateus likes how I drive. I'll pretend I'm in my Mustang."

Mateus gave a small groan and said, "Great. If A Empresa doesn't kill us, Tay's driving will. Next item, amigos. What about leaving Angola? How do we get back to the USA? Muni, can you work your magic? False IDs, dummy itineraries, the whole nine yards?"

The hacker's grin was sharp and feral. "Who do you think you're talking to, padawan? I'll have you set up with a digital smokescreen so thick, even the NSA would have trouble seeing through it." Muni paused, satisfied. "I've already been working on Romiana's visa. There is now a student visa in place for her. She's enrolled in San Jacinto Junior College in Houston. I hope you like history, Romiana."

"History is fine with me, but if we don't hurry, we'll be history. We need to leave right away before they get more teams involved. As time goes by, they'll bring in the government authorities. Time's not our friend."

"Muni, seems like you knew she was going with us before I did. Talk to us about the pros and cons of leaving via Lubango verses Luanda from your perspective," said Mateus.

"From Lubango you can go to Luanda or multiple cities in Angola.

The only international flight available is to Windhoek, Namibia, a short jaunt south from where you are. Tickets will not be a problem. The next flight to Windhoek is in about six hours."

Mateus said, "Going through Namibia means two security inspections, two immigration processes, two customs processes. I don't like the sound of that. But going back to Luanda means giving them plenty of time to mobilize all of their support, including the government."

"I'm with you," Tay replied. "We need to get our act together and run for the airport here. Lubango Airport or bust, buddy. Romiana?"

"*Sí,* I agree. We need to move. Lubango."

"We're unanimous," Mateus said. "Next issue. How will we transport the diamonds? The obvious way to do this, from a person who has watched his share of drug smuggling movies, is to sew them into the suitcase lining. The other alternative is to tape them to our bodies underneath our clothes. Neither makes me feel too good. We could mail all of them to ourselves, but that feels worse."

"Or we could find another old church and re-hide them," Tay said.

Mateus smiled slightly. "Ughh . . . other ideas?"

"I would stay simple, distribute them in the carry-on luggage and clothing. They won't show up on airport security scanners," said Muni, who had previously looked into the topic.

"Agreed," said Romiana.

"It sounds risky, but I think it's our best bet," Mateus said. "Romiana, can you get us three carry-on bags and some bulky clothes? We also need some sewing supplies." Romiana nodded and was out the door. "Muni, get on those tickets."

The next few hours were a blur of activity. They split the diamonds among themselves and concealed them, donned disguises with the new clothes, and rehearsed cover stories. They piled into a nondescript sedan and made it to the Lubango Airport, a half-dome structure with baby blue trim. Each of them carried a small, worn suitcase filled with inexpensive shirts and shorts, trying to blend in with the travelers.

Romiana and Tay exited first by pre-arrangement. They held hands as they walked toward the terminal. This sent an unexpected pang of jealousy through Mateus, which he knew was silly. In a strange way, he welcomed the feeling of jealousy, as it was a new emotion to him.

Mateus waited ten minutes, grabbed his suitcase and carry-on to follow, the weight of his carry-on, and the sticky tension in his mid-section reminding him of the diamonds and what was at stake. He approached the airport door.

Romiana and Tay were coming out of the airport terminal, faces ashen and eyes wide. They were no longer holding hands but retreating in a nervous shuffle. Mateus turned and followed discreetly behind them. They gathered back at the car and hurriedly threw the bags into the trunk, and Mateus lay down in the back once again.

"Our faces," Romiana gasped as she threw herself into the passenger seat. "They're everywhere. Wanted posters, small billboards. Ilidio's pulled out all the stops."

Tay gunned the engine, knuckles white against the steering wheel. "We need to move, now. If they've got the airports locked down then—"

He didn't need to finish the thought. They all knew what it meant. Their window was closing; the jaws of the trap were snapping shut with every passing second.

CHAPTER 34
LUBANGO BUMPER CARS

Lubango, Angola, January 17, 2010

Horátio Ilidio gritted his teeth as the paramedics eased him into the waiting ambulance, the searing pain in his shoulder a constant reminder of Mateus's handiwork. The wounded crime lord already had wheels in motion to get his revenge, orders barked into a blood-stained phone. He would not underestimate this American boy again.

These computer hackers would fail this time because he was going old school. No-fly alerts and even police arrest orders could be doctored and changed on computerized systems. With his connections and the concessionaire's help, he simply had hard copy pictures posted everywhere—airline terminals, railroad stations, taxi ranks, police stations. The posters showed the three of them, taken from a security camera download, and promised a substantial reward for information leading to their arrest. Once the police had them in custody, Ilidio would take over.

Lying in his hospital bed with an IV sticking out of his arm, Ilidio received word of a sighting at the Lubango Airport. Someone saw the trio leaving in a hurry. His heart raced as he quickly called in backup. They were heading for Namibia; he knew it.

But he would be waiting. And this time no quarter given; no clemency offered. The diamonds would be his.

Mateus sprawled across the back seat, clinging to the door handle as Tay raced their battered sedan through the streets of Lubango. Romiana rode shotgun, brows furrowed as she scanned alleyway openings and mirrors for any sign of pursuit.

After the airport fiasco, they had hurriedly stripped the diamonds from their sweaty bodies and got them into the duffel bag and trunk once again. They needed to get out of Lubango and into the anonymous countryside.

The plan was simple, born out of their desperation—run like hell for the Namibian border and try to stay one step ahead of A Empresa. Five hours to the border town of Oshikango, and then another seven to Windhoek, the capital of Namibia.

The old white Ford rushed down the main street in Lubango. Life filled the sidewalks, with people selling food and clothes, walking, laughing, kids chasing worn-out soccer balls.

Tay saw it first—a beat-up gray car racing out of the alley to their left, heading toward them at high speed. The car pointed straight at Tay, aiming for the driver's side door. Time seemed to slow to a crawl as he instinctively hit the accelerator and violently turned the wheel, a squeal of rubber as their car leaped forward. It was not nearly enough.

Metal screamed and glass exploded as the gray car impacted their back left rear panel with a violent crunch. The impact sent them spinning like a child's top, Mateus cracking his skull hard against the door. Stars in his eyes, his addled brain having a brief vision of diamonds cascading out of the trunk with soccer kids running over to scoop them up by the handful.

Tay lurched against Romiana but was able to keep his head up. He saw the gray car moving forward after the impact, pushing past their car. The gray car's brakes screamed as it skidded up and onto the sidewalk. A sickening thud as the gray car plowed into pedestrians. Women and children crushed by the car, before it continued into a ferocious head-on collision with a solid brick building. A paused shock. And then the screaming began.

People ran toward the accident from all directions, some to help the wounded, and others to pull the guilty driver from the car for punishment. Fists and kicks. Mob justice. Tay was not sure the man would survive.

Tay came to his senses and hit the accelerator hard again. They were all thrown back into the vinyl seats. There was no time to process all of this, as the next threat appeared. A white BMW and a hulking silver SUV were closing in on them at high speed.

Tay's eyes blazed with a mixture of concentration and fear. He took a sudden left turn into an alley, threading the needle with tires squealing and passengers barely holding on. While he sped off down the alley, their surprised pursuers hit the brakes and turned simultaneously into uncontrolled skids.

The BMW's suspension bounced, but the vehicle stayed right on their tail. The SUV was not so lucky, slamming into a corner building with such force that its un-seatbelted occupants catapulted through the front windshield and tumbled across unforgiving pavement.

Tay drove on with frenzied intensity and skill. He navigated blindly the side-streets and back alleys, maneuvering through the twists and turns so quickly that Mateus felt his stomach churn. The BMW followed, inexorable. Getting closer.

"It's time to discourage them, buddy," Tay said calmly, as if they were walking across the Cal Tech campus grounds together.

Mateus nodded grimly and retrieved the pistol from under his seat. He was not a good shot, and he knew it. Then add in a moving car, potholed roads, and nerves into the mix.

His magazine held seventeen shots. Seventeen chances to buy them just a little more time. Window opened, he carefully clicked off the safety. Leaning out, he rested his left elbow on the door frame for stability. He squeezed the trigger, recoil slamming up his arm like a jackhammer. Once, twice, three times. Then three more. Most of the shots pinged harmlessly off asphalt.

Mateus was not sure, but he didn't think any of them connected amidst all the bouncing around and his rotten aim. Frustrated, he started shooting again, wildly, the shots banging out. And then, a miracle. The pursuer's windshield shattered in a spider's web of cracks. The car swerved drunkenly, tires screaming as it spun out in a cloud of smoke.

They raced away, not lingering to see who or what they had hit inside the car. Mateus took stock, only three shots left for whatever or whoever was in front of them on this perilous ride.

"Good shootin', Tex," a smiling Tay said. "Only took you fourteen shots to hit something."

Mateus allowed himself a small grin as he carefully put the safety back on. He felt strangely buzzed, energized, with no C-4 coffee or cocaine as fuel. Not only had he taken decisive action, but he had put a bit of distance between them and that homicidal crime lord. It was unbelievable. Even more so was that the smart, beautiful, talented, sparkly eyed woman in the passenger seat seemed to like him.

They heard a loud rattle and crunchy noise coming from the back fender where it had been hit. It did not seem to slow them down yet.

"Guys, this is getting more dangerous by the minute. Should we give up the diamonds, make a deal, get ourselves to safety?" Mateus asked.

"No." Romiana's voice was a whip crack, turning towards him with intense eyes. "We see this through, Mateus. To whatever end."

"We're all in, man, and we're not stopping for anything. These diamonds are going to make a big difference," Tay said.

Mateus pondered for several heartbeats and asked, "Tay, what do you mean by a big difference?"

"What we've seen here for the past week. Poverty, people needing help, kids who are hungry. We've also seen some of the most beautiful, the most amazing people in the world. These diamonds put you—put us—in a position to help. In a position to make a difference."

Tay continued, "I know you, Mateus. You're not a guy who wants a huge house and a Maserati. You're going to want to make a difference."

This was why Tay was his best friend. He knew what Mateus wanted, even before he did himself. Tay was right about everything. The Angolan people were amazing and making a difference here was perfect, perhaps the antidote to a lonely professorship. There would be challenges, but they could help provide clean water, medicine, food, and clothing. The options were endless.

He was all in.

CHAPTER 35
A NIGHT AT THE PENSÃO

Xangogo, Angola, January 18, 2010

The sedan limped into the outskirts of Xangogo, its engine sputtering and groaning, a trail of leaking oil on the asphalt. As the trio exchanged weary glances, a million bright stars adorned the sky. It was past midnight, and past time to grab a room, regroup, and get a bit of rest before the final push to Namibia. They surveyed the sleepy town, its streets deserted, and storefronts shuttered.

"We need to stop," Tay said, voice thick with weariness. "Just for a few hours. Enough to catch our breath and let the car cool down."

Romiana nodded, her head lolling against the passenger seat headrest. "There's a *pensão* up ahead. Looks quiet, out of the way. Should be safe enough for a quick rest."

Mateus hesitated, the weight of the diamonds in the trunk a constant presence. The allure of a soft bed and a moment's respite were too powerful to resist. "Okay, but we take turns keeping watch. And we're back on the road before sunrise."

The Pensão Escola was a ramshackle affair, its whitewashed walls dingy with age and neglect, its tin roof rusty with visible holes. Romiana slipped from the car and made her way to the front desk, her gait steady despite her exhaustion.

The hotel clerk was a tired looking woman, her graying hair concealed in a makeshift turban of colorful orange and black African fabric, with thin-frame glasses perched on her nose above suspicious eyes. She watched Romiana approach with condescension, thinking, *A single woman checking in at this hour?*

"A single room, please," Romiana said, sliding a handful of crumpled bills across the pockmarked counter. "Just for one night."

The woman's gaze flicked from Romiana's face to the money and back again, her lips pursed in silent judgment. But she took the cash all the same, sliding a tarnished key across the counter with a grunt.

Romiana had opted for a solo check-in to prevent potentially alerting A Empresa. She walked from the tiny reception area outside, driving their car to a parking spot just outside the doorway to their room. The clerk continued to watch Romiana through holes in the faded drapes. Her suspicions were confirmed when she saw two additional shapes scurry from the car into the room. She picked up an ancient rotary dial phone on her weather-beaten desk and began dialing.

The room was a study in faded squalor—peeling wallpaper, threadbare carpets, a sagging mattress that had seen better days. It had not seen a vacuum cleaner in a long time. But to the bone-weary travelers, it might as well have been the Ritz.

Mateus and Tay collapsed onto the bed in a tangle of limbs, the springs creaking. Romiana curled up in the room's lone chair, her knees drawn to her chest and her eyes already fluttering closed.

But even as sleep threatened to claim him, Mateus forced himself to sit up, his voice rough with exhaustion. "We need to be ready," he mumbled, scrubbing at his face with calloused hands. "In case they find us."

They worked quickly; their movements sluggish but purposeful. The car moved out and to the back of the hotel. They dragged the dresser and nightstand in front of the door, creating a makeshift barricade. They jimmied open the bathroom window; the latch giving way with a rusty shriek.

Preparations made, Mateus and Tay lay on top of the covers of the small bed. Deep sleep came almost instantly. Romiana fought to stay awake as the first night watch, curled up in the room's only chair. At 3 a.m., they all came awake in an instant.

The tremendous crack at the front door was like a thunderclap, the flimsy door buckling inwards and splinters showering the air. Two A Empresa gunmen were bashing against the door with their shoulders. The dresser and nightstand held momentarily but were beginning to yield. Excitement overtook one gunman who pulled the trigger and unleashed two earsplitting blasts through the door and into the room.

The bullets splashed against the back wall as the trio rose frantically to their feet. Gunfire erupted behind them, prompting a panicked scramble toward the bathroom window. The diamonds were tossed out first, the precious gems landing with a muffled thud on the dirt outside. Then, one by one, they followed, clambering through the narrow opening to escape the hail of bullets.

Romiana was through the bathroom window, landing cat-like on the packed earth below. Tay followed with a similar landing while Mateus brought up the rear. The ground rushed up to meet him, the impact driving the air from his lungs in a whoosh. They had just cleared the window as the gunmen burst into the room.

And then they were running, half-stumbling, toward the car they'd carefully positioned close to the window. Romiana threw herself behind the wheel, the engine roaring to life as Tay and Mateus piled into the backseat with the duffel, a tangle of limbs and frantic curses.

Romiana hit the accelerator hard, and the back wheels spun, sending up a rooster tail of dirt and pebbles. A gun appeared outside the bathroom window, and the rear windshield exploded inward, a hail of glass raining down on them.

They were moving now, skidding and swerving but moving. More shots were fired their way. Bullets slammed into the trunk, the doors, and somehow even into the roof.

And then, miraculously, they were free. The car burst onto the road in a spray of gravel, Romiana fighting the wheel as they fishtailed wildly. Finally, the tires gained traction, and the car shot forward, leaving the danger behind. They looked back, anxious, but had made it away before the pursuit could get organized. Tay whooped in defiance, his head thrown back and his fists raised in victory.

Mateus sat motionless, body quivering, as he silently wondered what was next.

CHAPTER 36
RACING FOR WINDHOEK

Angola-Namibia Border, January 18, 2010

Horátio Ilidio's grip on the phone tightened as he took a calming breath and shook his head. The concessionaire Vicente was on the other end of the phone, his tirade ear-blistering. Even with the phone six inches away from Ilidio's ear, he could clearly hear Vicente's yelling.

"Listen closely, you *filho da puta*," Vicente snarled. "The MPLA platoon is en route to the border, but you will be there, large and in charge. You were a general, so be a general and command them. I don't give a shit about your little flesh wound. And how'd you miss them at the hotel? Unbelievable. Now do something right for a change. Get me my diamonds!"

Ilidio gritted his teeth. Again, with the *"my diamonds"* he thought. "Yes, *chefe*."

"Fail me again and a bullet in the shoulder will be the least of your worries." The line went dead, leaving Ilidio to stew in an impotent rage. His *friend* in the government, Vicente, had been helpful for once, influencing the Angolan army brass to deploy soldiers to stop these damn diamond thieves.

Ilidio had been hard at work, the pain in his shoulder pushed down deep as he conjured a plan. There were several crossings into Namibia, but he had figured correctly that they were heading for Oshikango, the most direct route to Windhoek. The border there was closed, and there were wanted posters at every airline, bus, and rail terminal. Multiple A Empresa cars were out on the road hunting for them.

His driver had their Mercedes over seventy miles per hour as they raced for the border where he would join a platoon of his men. He reclined in the luxurious soft leather backseat and closed his eyes as the air conditioning blew hard on his face. The disgraced Tomé was with him in the back seat, quiet and subservient, but back working despite the screw up at the cathedral.

Ilidio allowed himself a small, vicious smile. The net was rapidly tightening on these belligerent treasure hunters. It would soon be game over.

Romiana fixed her eyes on the horizon as she guided their worn-out car down the rutted highway. They had stopped once for gas and snacks and were nearing the Namibian border. In the backseat, Mateus and Tay traded stories and laughter, talking about anything except diamonds and treasure.

"You see, guys, my people came from here," Tay said, voice soft with reverence. "I can feel it in my heart, my bones. This place, Angola, it's a part of me." He reached out, clasping Mateus's shoulder with a strong, warm grip. "And you Matty, you're my brother. Blood of my blood. Even here, a bullet hole in my shoulder, in a crashed and shot up car, I'm at peace." Mateus smiled broadly; his chest tight with emotion.

Tay grinned right back and continued. "And this is a special woman. Smart. Cool under pressure. And beautiful." He pointed at her and grinned again, warmly. "You're a part of this, Romiana. A part of us. We've been through so much, and the two of you have become connected, I hope forever."

Both Romiana and Mateus blushed. She started talking softly. "Forever sounds lovely," she said. "But my father's trying to kill us and I'm damaged goods, married before and then divorced." A long pause. "Another thing is that I can't seem to have children."

Mateus did not know what to say but reached out, his fingers brushing the nape of her neck in a tender gesture. "None of that matters, Romiana. Not to me."

Tay smiled at him, happy for his friend. "Matty, you can have it all, you know. Making a difference and helping people is possible with these diamonds. You can finish your degree and find the research that interests you. You can also have a family. Don't limit yourself."

Tay is right, Mateus thought. *Maybe I really can have it all.* "Tay, you seem to have a way that you—"

"No! Look!" Tay shouted.

Romiana swore under her breath, slamming hard on the brakes and sending them pitching forward. The trio sat in silence, looking at the border crossing. Namibia was in sight, so close. Immigration officials sat in a squat, nondescript dirty white building, peeling paint, with a barbed wire topped chain-link fence.

This was expected, but arrayed in front of the gates like a nightmare was a platoon of soldiers. They had grim faces and were heavily armed with weapons pointed directly at them. Flanking them were two armored personnel vehicles with mounted machine guns.

Mateus felt his stomach drop, a leaden weight, even as his mind raced with options. *Give up. Not a chance. Go back to Luanda. Locate an alternate crossing point into Namibia.* In desperation, Mateus looked down at his pistol, realizing the absurdity of thinking of a fight with three bullets.

Tay looked behind them and could see a Jeep bearing down on them. A pincer movement by Ilidio, reliving his days as a UNITA general. They did not have time for discussion. They did not have time for anything.

Tay's voice, tight with urgency, shattered the stunned silence. "There's a dirt track east of the checkpoint. If we can slip past the cordon—"

Romiana nodded grimly, jaw clenched with determination. "Hold on to your butts, boys. This is going to get bumpy."

She gripped the steering wheel tight and floored the accelerator, pulling off the highway toward the dirt road. The car bucked and shuddered, dirt and gravel flying as they bounced over potholes and gullies.

Mateus risked a glance backward, heart in his throat. The soldiers hadn't given chase, and the Jeep had stopped at the highway. There was no pursuit. His brows furrowed in confusion.

Tay said, "What the hell is going on? They're not going to just let us go."

Romiana said nothing but simply drove on in silence as she tried to keep their desired direction along a maze of dirt roads and trails. The savanna rushed past in a haze of heat and dust.

"We're almost there!" she cried in relief, pointing.

Back at the border crossing, Ilidio was watching his diamonds fade into the distance. "Go after them!" he yelled, face an angry mask and fists clenched. Tomé was standing motionless next to him holding an AK-47.

The cloud of dust was fading into the distance, and no one was following. The soldiers backed away from Ilidio, reluctance and fear on their faces as they moved from this madman. They all looked toward the fleeing vehicle and knew it was heading into the border mine fields.

The squad's sergeant, cautioned, "Generalissimo, it is too risky to go off-road in this area. The ground here is full of mines, sir." Angola, with its staggering two thousand mine fields and fifteen million landmines, was the most heavily mined country in the world. The sergeant and every soldier here had friends who were missing a foot or a leg from an encounter with a mine.

Ilidio grabbed Tomé and the sergeant by their necks, one in each hand, and forcefully dragged them to the nearest Jeep. He shoved the sergeant into the driver's seat and jumped in beside him, leaving Tomé with the backseat.

"Drive!"

Romiana's car ran over a spot, undisturbed for decades. The weight of the vehicle's right front tire depressed the old pressure plate, which drove the firing pin into the detonator. Immediately, the main explosive charge of the anti-personnel mine exploded. In an instant, the world turned upside down.

The explosion was deafening. A 150-gram Russian PMA-2 landmine pushed upward with a percussive blast. Metal shards lifting the right front end of the car and driving metal, glass, and splintered engine parts through the shattered firewall and into the cabin. In a surreal, almost dreamlike sequence, the car began its unhurried tumble, executing one full revolution, then another, before finally coming to rest upside down.

Mateus felt the explosion as a full body slam, the noise and force hitting his body like a sledgehammer. Lifted from his seat, the seatbelt digging into his chest with bruising force as the car flipped. The smell of smoke filled his nostrils. Held upside down by his seatbelt, his dark hair hung down, and his eyes watched the pistol lying on the ceiling, spinning slowly. Then the hiss of ruptured hoses. Tinny ping of settling metal.

Mateus thought the soldiers had followed them and used a bazooka or a howitzer to hit them. Glass was everywhere except in the windows, with pieces in their hair, clothes, and on the ceiling. Mateus fumbled for the release. He dropped awkwardly to the roof of the car and out the window. Romiana was already standing.

"Tay?" he croaked, voice raw and ragged in his own ears. No reply. They rushed to the passenger side of the vehicle. Romiana let out a gasp. There was blood leaking out from the door and onto the ground.

Mateus scrambled across the shattered glass, heedless of cuts and scrapes on his hands and knees. Tay lay crumpled against the door, his eyes closed and his face a mask of blood.

"No," Mateus whispered, working at his friend's seatbelt with shaking fingers. He jerked and heaved and was able to get the door open, to get his hands on his friend. Romiana was at his side in an instant, her own injuries forgotten as she helped ease Tay's limp form from the wreckage. They gently removed him and lay him down, Tay's breathing was shallow and his face pale. They heard a sound in the distance, the roar of an approaching vehicle.

"Tay, can you hear me?" A Jeep was getting closer, but he did not care. Tay's eyes fluttered and then were still. Mateus ripped Tay's bloody shirt open, looking for wounds and prepared to construct a makeshift bandage.

Romiana crawled into the upside-down vehicle and grabbed the pistol, her face a mask of grim resolve. She rose and took up a combat stance, knees slightly bent, holding the pistol with two hands, braced behind the upside-down car.

The approaching vehicle came closer, and she could see her father. Even from here he looked unhinged, gray hair wild and arms gesturing and pointing. *"Andale cabrão! Andale!"*

Ilidio had found them.

The Jeep skidded to a halt, and the men piled out in a flurry of dust and shouted orders. Ilidio strode forward, eyes wide. At his side, Tomé's AK-47 pointed straight at them.

"Fire!" Ilidio screamed, spittle flying from his lips. "Shoot! Shoot! Shoot!"

But Tomé hesitated, the barrel of his weapon wavering. The general turned to face him, rage on his face. Finally, the shots came. Tomé fired, a burst of thirty shots that crackled through the air.

Ilidio had seen a lot of war and heard plenty of gunfire and AK-47 rounds. He knew with certainty that these shots had gone high, very high, twenty feet over the heads of their target. His face changed as a new realization came to him. He gave Tomé a knowing glare, lips tight and eyebrows low.

Romiana flinched and instinctively ducked as Tomé's bullets flew over her head. Then she stood, back ramrod straight and face a mask of determination. It was not much of a contest, her three bullets against an AK-47, but it was this. crazy defiance or wait to be killed.

Even with all that had gone on between them, Romiana hesitated. Killing her father was difficult to fathom, despite his evil nature and abuse. With steely determination, Horátio Ilidio was squarely in her sights.

The pistol barked once, twice, three times, each volley missing its mark. She was out of bullets. She threw the gun to the side, disgustedly.

Ilidio lunged forward and snatched the AK-47 from Tomé, ready to kill his own daughter and these two American fools.

CHAPTER 37
SHOTS FIRED

Angola-Namibia Border, January 18, 2010

Mateus was standing now, beside Romiana. He gently reached over and took her hand. Their eyes met, a wordless exchange of love and acceptance as they prepared for the end. Romiana gave his hand a squeeze, a silent prayer for them and what might have been.

The world narrowed to a single, crystalline moment as Ilidio leveled the AK-47 at them, his scarred face twisted in triumph. Beside him, Tomé stood impassive, a silent sentinel awaiting the inevitable. The sergeant on his left looked uncertain, eyes wide at this scene.

"You've both caused me nothing but trouble." Ilidio gestured with the rifle he had seized. "You, for the last two weeks, and you for your entire life. Make your peace with whatever gods you pray to."

Mateus saw the scar on Ilidio's face seeming to pulse red as he prepared to shoot. Then he felt Romiana let go of his hand.

Even as the last words left Ilidio's lips, Romiana was moving. With a surprising burst of speed, she lunged forward, a desperate sprint toward her father and the weapon. Arms pumping, her steps rapidly closed the sandy ground between them. But Ilidio was too far, much too far away. The AK-47 barked, a staccato burst of fire and smoke that was deafening even in the open air.

Romiana jerked and danced, her body shuddering as the bullets tore into her. And then she crumpled to the ground on her back, blood-soaked. Her face was serene, eyes wide and staring, as if disconnected from all the carnage below.

Mateus ran to her. In desperation, he prepared to try some frantic CPR and then saw the wounds clearly. This was beyond CPR, beyond a doctor and ambulance, far beyond anything.

His mind reeling, Mateus gathered her in his arms, heedless of the gun trained at him. Sobs racked his frame, and he began to tremble and shake. A mountain of diamonds was not worth this. What have I done?

"You're next, *mi amigo*. Revenge at last on your *cabrão* grandfather. The diamonds will be mine again." Ilidio's laugh was triumphant but hoarse and raw, all jagged edges difficult to the listeners.

Mateus stood to meet his fate, closing his eyes, crossing himself, as he prepared for bullets. The barrel of the AK rose to center on Mateus's chest.

A single shot rang out. Mateus felt no pain but clutched at his heart anyway. He opened his eyes and looked down. No blood. Time seemed to stall, and he looked up to see a panorama of three men.

Tomé was standing still as a statue, arm outstretched, a smoking 9mm pistol in his hand. Ilidio stood with a small hole in his temple, a trickle of blood rolling down his ruined cheek. The sergeant stood still in absolute shock, his face covered with Ilidio's blood, brain, and bits of skull.

The scene was a tableau of horror, a macabre sculpture, frozen and timeless, until Ilidio broke the spell, collapsing like a broken accordion down to the Angolan dirt.

Tomé ran the few steps to the lifeless form of Romiana. He started to kneel when Mateus shouted, "Tomé!"

Mateus pointed frantically at the sergeant. The MPLA soldier was bringing up his pistol to bear on Tomé.

Tomé rolled gracefully and came up on one knee. The sergeant's gun barked twice just as he reached this position, the crack of the soldier's gun piercing the air. Adrenaline and Luanda street-bred toughness kept Tomé going. He fired back once, and then again. The sergeant fell without a sound into the bloody dirt beside a dead General Horátio Ilidio.

Tomé dropped his gun and crawled to Romiana, blood leaking out onto the sand. He cradled her bloody, dead body in his hands. Tears streamed, mixing with their blood. He collapsed beside her, gasping for air.

"You loved her?" Mateus said softly, shocked and confused.

"*Idiota*, I used to be her husband." Without another word, Tomé turned over and lay on his back beside Romiana. He was still then, the last few heaves of his chest marking the end.

Mateus could only stare. The impact of losing Romiana had hit him like an invisible wall. He didn't know how long he knelt there beside her, lost in a haze of grief and recrimination in the African sun.

A part of his locked-down brain awoke enough to shout, "Tay!" He had somehow forgotten about his friend. Mateus rushed back to Tay, afraid that he was going to lose him too.

He knelt beside Tay. Fear, cold, and dread settled in his gut as he took in the blood-soaked fabric of Tay's shirt, the ashen pallor of his face. Mateus could see the slight rise and fall of his chest, a regular rhythm. He was alive, if only just.

Examining him, he could see that there were no new wounds or gaping holes, just the torn stitches from the earlier gunshot wound. It was all too much, and tears of relief flowed silently down Mateus's cheeks.

"I'm not done yet, Matty," Tay rasped, his voice little more than a windy whisper. "Just . . . just give me a minute to catch my breath."

CHAPTER 38
THE WILD, WILD WEST

Oshikango, Namibia, January 20, 2010

The dingy walls of their motel room in Oshikango seemed to close in on Mateus. He lay on a lumpy mattress, eyes bloodshot and heavy with the weight of unshed tears, the peeling wallpaper and water-stained ceiling a mocking reminder of just how far he had fallen.

Sleep had become a distant memory, a luxury lost from the gaping void that Romiana's death. *What could I have done differently?* He felt crushed and empty, all desire gone, his insides a mushy mess.

Beside him, Tay tossed and turned, his own grief a palpable presence in the stifling air. The cacophony of street noise—raucous laughter, drunken shouts, and the occasional gunshot—filtered through the paper-thin walls, a jarring counterpoint to their pain.

Mateus thought back to those final, horrific moments at the border. Ilidio's sneering grin. Tomé's redemption. Romiana's bloody body. It felt like a cruel nightmare. With trembling fingers, Mateus had gently placed his mother's jet-black rosary in Romiana's hand and kissed her gently on the forehead. Then, he and Tay had needed to move, worried that the rest of the soldiers would come to exact revenge.

It had been a nervous one hundred yards to the border. Each step was a game of Russian roulette as they picked their way through the minefield. Mateus's mental calculation on what would happen if they had stepped on another anti-personnel mine was not pretty. And he decided not to share that thought with Tay.

Mateus had insisted on going first, diamond duffel bag on his shoulder, with Tay following at a ten-foot interval, stepping in Mateus's footprints. Tay had a fresh bandage on his shoulder and could walk, albeit very slowly, to the border town. Mateus had been surprised he could walk at all, but the blood from the ripped open stitches looked worse than it was, and the concussion from the crash was something he seemed to shake off.

Their cheap hotel in Oshikango was called The Bird House. They spent several days there in recovery and grief and restless sleep. A general exhaustion had set in from all they had been through, coupled with feelings of loss.

This was a hazy time. Mateus had not eaten and had been losing weight, his slim frame not well suited for weight loss. Tay forced him to drink Gatorade to keep him hydrated. They had called Muni, really just to hear her voice, a calming lifeline, and to ask about the city.

"Well, boys, Oshikango is no joke. Obviously, it's on the border with Angola," Muni warned, her voice filled with concern. "Angolans come across the border for sex and alcohol, maybe not in that order. You'll see that prices are way cheaper than in Luanda, because of the much lower taxes. So, smuggling beer and other stuff back across the border is a good way to make money. It's a very rough place. Watch your butts, gentlemen." They talked a bit longer, both men enjoying the sound of her voice and the promise of normalcy it embodied.

It was evening, and a racket of loud shouts and louder music were coming through the walls, surrounding them. *Cucashops*, named after a Portuguese beer, were plentiful in Oshikango. Their hotel was near two rowdy *cucashops* called *'Da Ghetto'* and *'Livin the Life'*.

On multiple occasions, Tay and Mateus had spoken quietly together during these foggy days. Tay's was a voice of comfort and of reason. He spoke of how none of this was Mateus's fault.

It was time to plan their next moves. They were far from airports and the US, hauling a sack of diamonds in a rough border town. They needed to go.

They settled on Cape Town, which was twenty-two hours away. It had multiple international flights. They agreed on the destination and called Muni.

"Muni, we need your help again. We're planning to head for Cape Town but don't have a car and are almost out of money," said Mateus. "We're thinking that there might be diamond dealers here. What do you think about us selling a small portion of the diamonds here to fund our travel and living expenses?"

"I've already looked at that." Mateus could almost see her satisfied smile from six thousand miles away. She loved being one step ahead. "There are two dealers in Oshikango who buy illegal diamonds. Unfortunately, both are pretty protective and don't like to deal with outsiders. They're also both quite dangerous."

"Got it, won't talk to us and are very dangerous. Great combination. What kind of wizard are you?" said Tay.

"It is what it is, my young hobbits."

"We're going to have to sell these diamonds at some point. Might as well start here," said Mateus.

"Okay. You'll need to watch yourselves. I would only sell the minimum in Oshikango. The diamond prices you have in your head are about forty or fifty percent higher than what you'll get there. Start now and lower your expectations."

"Thanks Muni. Good advice." Talking to the other beautiful woman in Mateus's life brought his mind back to Romiana, and he fell silent, head down.

Tay saw this and took over. "We're on the same page. We only want to sell enough to have money for a car, airline tickets, and some spending cash. What's the name of the least objectionable of these bozos, and where can we find him?"

"His name is Warinhenga. He lives above the From da North

cucashop about three blocks from where you are. He's a hard case, but your best chance of unloading some of those diamonds without getting your throat cut."

"Muni, you're the best." Tay said.

"Be safe in the cucashop boys. Think 'Mos Eisley cantina' danger levels."

"Even I know that one. Be cool, Muni." Tay hung up.

Mateus pulled himself together, and the two of them got ready. They had taken pistols and ammunition from Tomé and the dead soldier. These were stuffed in the back waistband of their pants, their shirts untucked to hide the bulge. Ready to go, they headed toward From da North to meet Warinhenga.

CHAPTER 39
OF KNIVES & NEGOTIATIONS

Oshikango, Namibia, January 21, 2010

The pulsing beat of the hip-hop *kwaito* music washed over them as Mateus and Tay approached From da North. The house-music style rap, punched up with African percussion, was loud, and the place was lively and raucous.

Inside, the air was thick with the stench of cheap booze and cheaper perfume, the interior illuminated with the glow of flickering fluorescent bulbs. Truck drivers and young men filled the room, some playing cards and all drinking hard, while they pawed at scantily clad women, their faces flushed with drink and lust.

Young women with too much make-up, with skirts too short, circulated and spoke in whispers with the men. Appointments and arrangements were made. Mateus shook his head, not from any morality qualms, but knowing from Muni that the rampant sex trade in Oshikango had led to an alarming prevalence of HIV in the area.

Mateus and Tay shouldered their way to the bar, their senses on high alert as they scanned the room for any sign of trouble. The bartender, a squat, pock-faced man with a stained apron stretched tight across an ample belly, eyed them with distrust.

Mateus raised his index finger to bring the man to them. Before the bartender could respond, a fight broke out at one table. Cards and money flew in every direction, as wild haymaker punches were thrown, and one prostitute was flung hard against the wall.

The bartender watched all this calmly, his expression one of weariness. "Outside!" he bellowed, his voice cutting through the *kwaito* music and the noise. On cue, a hulking brute of a man in a gray, ripped Yale sweatshirt emerged from the shadows at the end of the bar. He carried an oversized, scarred baseball bat club in one meaty fist as he waded into the chaos. In moments, the situation calmed, and several instigators were thrown unceremoniously out into the street.

The bartender turned his attention to Mateus, eyes narrowing in suspicion.

"We need to speak with Señor Warinhenga," Mateus said, his voice projecting more confidence than he felt. "It's in his best interests to talk with us. Umm . . . he'll want to speak with us." Mateus remained stoic, trying to look like a serious individual.

The bartender shook his head "*no*" in reflex, but then hesitated, looking hard at these two strangers. Warinhenga owned this cucashop and was his boss. The man absolutely hated being bothered. The outsider wasn't well dressed and didn't look like the criminal type. Still, this guy spoke like someone with intelligence, and he had a gravity to him.

A one-hundred-dollar bill appeared suddenly in Mateus's hand and was smoothly passed across to the bartender. The bartender nodded, reassured by the amount. This was enough for the squat man to take a chance with Warinhenga.

"Follow me," he grunted, and led them up a narrow staircase with worn wooden treads.

At the top of the stair, a wiry man with tired eyes stood guard, his hand resting lightly on the butt of a holstered pistol. After a few whispered words from the bartender, the guard frowned and nodded. He ushered Mateus and Tay through an old wooden door, covered in peeling green paint, and down a dimly lit hallway. The walls were an aged and cracked, pale blue, while the ceiling had two single light bulbs hanging from their electrical cords.

The door at the end of the hall swung open, revealing a spacious office that was at odds with the barroom squalor below. Antique furniture and plush carpets spoke of wealth and power, the trappings of a man who had clawed his way to the top.

And there, behind a large wooden, antique European desk, looking every inch the successful business owner, sat Warinhenga himself. Hair oiled and slicked straight back from his forehead. Well-tailored pinstriped suit. Colorful pink paisley bowtie. He stared at them with a predatory gleam through almost closed lids.

The safe behind Warinhenga captivated Mateus. An old ornate safe with four separate dials. The black door of the safe was painted with gold swirling art déco flourishes and had a small badge saying, *Made by F.L. Silva Almeida.* Mateus wondered how many diamonds had passed through its interior over the years.

A second guard sat near the door on a wooden chair, a pistol across his lap and an AK-47 leaning against him. His scowling face greeted them, and he patted the machine gun in welcome. The fierce man brusquely frisked them. He easily found and removed the two pistols, giving them a disdainful smirk, and then forcefully pushed them down into two chairs.

The chairs were low, with the back legs shorter than the front. It was an old trick, but an effective one. Their heads were a foot lower than Warinhenga's, forced to lean slightly back, which was uncomfortable and disconcerting. All this was to the headman's advantage, of course.

Mateus took a steadying breath, mind racing for the right words. "Señor Warinhenga, thank you very much for seeing us. We hope to do some business with you, not just today, but as a long-term partner." Warinhenga sat, still as death, eyes closed in exasperation.

Suddenly on his feet, Warinhenga gave the bartender a brutal backhand across the face. "Why'd you bring me these little *comé mierdas* to my door?" Another slap. "You know I'm too busy for this!"

A third slap to the face. The bartender turned and fled, picking up a kick to his backside.

Mateus felt his own anger rising at the words as he thought of all they had been through. He took a breath and held it for a moment before exhaling slowly. Bending, he took off his left shoe, removed a small white folded handkerchief and placed it on the desk.

Mateus slowly and deliberately opened each corner to reveal five large, rough diamonds. As always with these Tundavala diamonds, a hush and pause of wonder. Even Warinhenga sat perfectly still, this experienced black-market diamond dealer, his normally half-closed eyes fully opened, with eyebrows raised. He recovered quickly.

"These are, well, adequate. Yes, adequate. I've seen better," Warinhenga said, voice thick with greed and not for a moment taking his eyes off the diamonds. "What do you want for them?"

Mateus and Tay sat stonily in silence. They were not willing to set the table in the negotiation by offering an initial price.

"Ha! You won't talk?" Warinhenga gave a greasy smile and reached for his jeweler's loupe. "May I?" he asked. Seeing Mateus's nod, he put the loupe up to his right eye and carefully examined each diamond. "How much?"

"As you can see, Señor Warinhenga, these diamonds grade out at a *D* color and *IF* for clarity with no inclusions. The highest quality. With a range of ten to fifteen carats, these are clearly rare diamonds of exceptional quality. The question is, how much will you pay for them?"

Warinhenga's face reddened, and he grimaced. A wicked-looking knife appeared as if by magic, and he slammed it into the top of the desk, the point a hair width away from Mateus's hand. The great wooden structure jumped at the impact and the dagger vibrated menacingly, one-half-inch of the long blade embedded below the desk surface.

"Name your price," he growled, his eyes flashing dangerously. "And pray that it's a reasonable one."

Mateus was silent for two heartbeats, feeling Tay tense beside him and knowing his friend was ready to spring into action. In the silence, Mateus studied the desktop closely, and reviewed the material properties of wood in his mind. One place was perfect for his purpose.

He quickly reached forward for the knife. Two distinct clicks from behind signaled the door guard's deadly intent, breaking the silence in the small office as the door guard took off the safeties. Guns now pointed at the back of his head, ready to fire.

Mateus slammed the knife into the desk with all of his might, directing all the force at his chosen place. Mateus hit the existing crack perfectly, and the knife went into the desk up to the hilt. The knife vibrated, blade imbedded in the warm wood. Warinhenga sat back a bit, eyes widening. Tay was stunned too, as the nerdy Mateus had never been known for his strength.

"Señor Warinhenga, we're going to be coming from Angola to Oshikango once a month. We have a steady source of diamonds. Our supplier is high up in the Angolan military." Mateus's eyes never left Warinhenga's face. "We want to work with you and will bring you larger shipments later. If we can get the right price today, we could have a bright future together." Tay and Mateus had worked up this idea to help raise the price but also to discourage him from simply taking the diamonds and killing them in this room.

Warinhenga thought hard, picking up one diamond to examine it again and to buy some time. Finally, he looked at the guard near the door, and gave a slight shake *no*. Mateus glanced back at the guard, whose shoulders relaxed as he sat back in the chair. For the first time, it seemed like they might make it out of here alive.

"Five thousand for the lot," Warinhenga said brusquely.

Mateus paused, as if in thought. "Our number is thirty-five. We can't go lower."

"Then our business is over before it has begun. You are overvaluing these. Look around you, my friends. You're in a cucashop in Namibia. You're not in Zurich or London. Prices here are more reasonable, more people-friendly, more business-friendly. I can come up to seven thousand only because I like you guys."

"These diamonds are of the highest quality, and we have a general to report back to. He will hurt us if we come back with less than thirty."

Warinhenga looked deeply offended and stood up to pace in front of the safe, stopping once to rub its surface. "Okay, I should not do this but ten thousand, final offer."

Mateus did not reply but stood up and folded the white cloth across the diamonds. Tay stood as well.

Warinhenga was back at the desk, a hand raised in a stopping motion. "Wait, wait, wait. Once a month, you say? With larger consignments?"

"Four or five times this many diamonds. Same or better quality. I should not tell you this, but we will have pink diamonds for you as well in the future. Let's shake hands at twenty-eight."

After twenty more minutes of tense negotiation, they made their way back to The Bird House hotel with twenty-one thousand dollars in their hands. This was a far cry from their worth, but enough for their needs.

By evening, they had a serviceable old Toyota Corolla, a change of clothes, and some used bags for the flight to the US. They did all this for around six thousand, leaving them with plenty for the trip. After dinner, they showered and sat on the edge of the bed together.

Tay clapped a hand on Mateus's shoulder with a fierce grin. "You did good back there, brother," he said, voice thick with emotion. "Romiana would be proud."

Mateus felt a lump in his throat at Romiana's name, but he pushed it down and said, "Let's just get our butts home."

CHAPTER 40
EPILOGUE

Altadena, California, August 29, 2010

The punch sped toward Mateus's face like a freight train, a blur of knuckles and power. He saw it as if in slow motion, on a flat trajectory toward his nose. A fluid half-step to the left took him just beyond the arc of the punch. He deflected the incoming punch with his left palm, and it sailed harmlessly past him. His opponent had over-committed and was leaning forward, off balance.

In that instant, Mateus struck with a right-leg front kick. This hit his adversary hard in the chest, and he crumpled to the ground, his breath coming out in a whoosh.

The tournament referee raised a white flag for one point, while Tay let out a huge whoop of approval from the sideline. Like Mateus, he wore a white martial arts *dobok* robe, with his black belt standing out in stark contrast against the fabric.

The last six months had been a time of immense change. Mateus had thrown himself into physical training with a fervor that bordered on obsession. Taekwondo, yoga, strength, conditioning. He pushed himself to the limits of his endurance, sculpting his body into a formidable weapon.

Mateus had completed his dissertation, a groundbreaking fusion of computer science and neurology that had earned him the coveted title of doctor. He was now Dr. Mateus de Silva. Mateus studied Mihaly Csikszentmihalyi religiously and got into the flow state the scholar described, with his physical, mental, and even spiritual sides merging into peak performance.

So, he trained. He studied. He poured himself into his work, his research, anything to keep the demons at bay. All the exhausting activity seemed to dull the Romiana-sized ache in his heart. He had even cut his cocaine usage, which made him feel good.

Back at the apartment in Altadena, working on his computer and drinking a strong C-4 coffee, Mateus looked over at the altar, the candles burning. His mother, Mariposa, was still in the center, but with an addition. A picture of Romiana was there, taken during their dinner on the *Ilha*, with her beaming smile and bright eyes staring fearlessly into the camera. It cheered Mateus to look at both of them.

Along with Muni, Tay and Mateus had researched and implemented a diamond sales plan. The three had looked at multiple options and strategies. They ended up splitting the diamond fortune into thirds.

They had sold the first third of the diamonds in South Africa prior to coming home. Johannesburg had a government-controlled, world-class diamond industry. Over the course of three weeks, they made contacts and could sell the diamonds at a reasonable price.

With another third, they traveled to New York City where their fortune could go unnoticed. There were Hasidic Jews willing to take the stones without the standard documentation. The dealers they targeted were a part of the city's Diamond District on 47th Street. These Orthodox Jews, originally fleeing Nazi Germany, set up shop in NYC and had been in business ever since. Mateus and Tay had walked down the street to the dealers, between 5th and 6th Avenue, surrounded by black hats and the Yiddish language.

They saved the best and brightest of the stones for the city of Surat in India. Silk City, The Diamond City, and The Green City were just a few of the names for Surat. It was the worldwide hub for diamond cutting and polishing. The city processed ninety percent of the world's diamonds.

They invested money to process their diamonds, a complex procedure that included cleaving and sawing, bruting, laser cutting, and final faceting and polishing. This was expensive but allowed them to get the absolute highest price.

Their Indian agent was outstanding, helping them manage the process and sell the final third of the diamonds. A tall, slim man with a striking black mustache, he remained calm even in the face of emotional and shouting diamond processors and buyers. A tremendous asset and friend to them, this man walked and acted so much like Mateus that Tay took to calling him Mateus's twin brother from a different mother.

In all they garnered four hundred and sixty million, a staggering sum and even higher than Mateus's initial estimate. Their work in India and the overall strategy had paid off. The money sat in Swiss and Cayman Islands bank accounts, safe from prying eyes. They were ready to fund their charitable foundation.

It was called the RIMAD Foundation, or the "Romiana Ilidio Making a Difference" foundation. Mateus was the executive director and Tay the chief operating officer. Muni's mother and Tay's father formed the rest of the governing board. Angola had touched them all, becoming a part of their lives. Mateus and Tay wanted to make a difference there.

A constant feature of street life in Luanda was the vision of women carrying containers of heavy water on their heads. They walked long distances to get the water and bring it back to their dirt-floored, tin-roofed homes. Mateus wanted to focus their initial efforts there. They would provide clean water for the people.

Mateus was sitting sat at his desk, working on water well designs for Angola, when his phone rang. His brow furrowed at the Cuban phone number.

"Aunt Dolores?" he said, voice tight with sudden, inexplicable dread.

"Nephew, we have a problem. I . . . I don't know how to say this." His aunt's voice was strained. "I was cleaning your grandmother's house so we could sell it. I found something, under a loose floorboard."

"What is it?" Mateus whispered.

"Another cigar box. And inside, a map, torn and stained with blood. The top of the map says *"Estoy Aqui"* (I'm Here). Mateus leaned back hard in his chair, eyes darting to the Jesus bust and the promise of the white powder within.

"There's a recent note from South Africa. It is signed by the colonel, Juan Mateus de Silva himself."

Dolores' voice quivered with emotion, her voice barely audible over the sudden roaring in his ears. "Your grandfather is alive, but he's in deep trouble. You have to come!"

ACKNOWLEDGMENTS

First and foremost, I would like to express my deepest gratitude to my wife, Lisa. Her unwavering love, patience, and support have made this book possible. Our countless conversations about the craft of writing, editing, and publishing were invaluable in shaping this work.

I am indebted to Tome Gime for his meticulous research in Luanda, providing vital details about the local cathedrals. My sincere thanks to Madeline Schmoll for her insightful consultation on coding-related matters.

I would also like to extend my appreciation to Glenn Hammett (*getgdesign.com*), Galip K. and Steve Royes (*walkthroughproductions.com*), whose efforts significantly improved and shaped the author's website associated with this book—(*www.jeffreykschmoll.com*).

This journey would not have been possible without the excitement and encouragement of numerous friends who fueled me to the finish line. Their belief in this project was a constant source of motivation.

My heartfelt thanks go to editors Jacquelin Cangro, Edmund Pickett, and the dedicated team of beta readers who helped refine the novel and elevate its quality. I am grateful to Koehler Books and my editor, Joe Coccaro, for invaluable contributions in bringing Tundavala to life.

www.ingramcontent.com/pod-product-compliance
Lightning Source LLC
LaVergne TN
LVHW041802060526
838201LV00046B/1093